The Blue Wildebeest

BY HELEN SPERBER

Grand Junction, Colorado

DISCLAIMER

This is a work of fiction. References to historical events, real people and real places are used fictitiously. Other names, characters, places and events are products of the author's imagination and any resemblance to actual people, places and events is coincidental. Descriptions of real places on Cape Cod are drawn from my memory, and are not necessarily accurate. The town and community of Shelton are purely fictional and not intended to resemble any real place on Cape Cod.

© Copyright 2017 Helen Sperber
All rights reserved in whole or in part.

ISBN: 978-0-9965828-5-8
Library of Congress Control Number: 2017932980
First Edition
Printed in the United States of America

Cover painting by Lori Powell

For more information contact:
Helen Sperber
hmsper@gmail.com
Visit website at helensperber.com

Acknowledgements

This book would not have happened without the support and encouragement of so many people in my life.

My children and grandchildren have believed in me even when I wanted to give up, providing computer support, editing, motivation, and space for mini-writing retreats, as well as constant encouragement.

My colleagues in The Colorado Chapter of Women Writing for (a) Change, have shared with me several semesters of struggling to write from the heart. In the process, this group has birthed some of my dearest friendships. Anne and Karen, thank you for facilitating the existence of this wonderful group.

Melba, those summer mornings and winter afternoons we spent visiting the ducks always sent me back to the keyboard with renewed determination. Your appreciation of my work has helped me slog through the rough days.

Barb, you inspired me by getting your own book completed and published. Thanks for sharing those weeklong personal writing retreats with me, including the "research" trip to Cape Cod. You always chuckled as I fought with my laptop, which would never behave as I wanted it to.

Prologue

As I grow deeper into my life,
closer to the time when
I will have run out of days,
the twin specters of broken body and crippled mind
evolve on the horizon.

They fill me, not with fear and dread,
but with fierce determination,
and a sense of great urgency
which overcomes my cautious nature.

At eighteen,
I saved myself (or not)
for my prince, my one true love.
He came, and went, it seems
in serial fashion.

Now, 50 years later,
for what
am I to save myself?

Waiting is no longer an option.
If I am to dance, it must be now.

PART ONE
THE BEGINNING

Chapter 1

"Sailing."

"Sailing?"

"Sure. Sailing. I'd like that. You know, like in the movies. Robert Redford."

"Who?"

"Oh, don't tell me you're too young to know Robert Redford." She gazed at the painting of a sailboat hanging above the fireplace. "Though I suppose he doesn't do the sailing anymore. He probably plays the old geezer running the bait shop now." Mattie paused. "Anyway, I'd love to go sailing. If I'm going to start a — What did you call it? A bucket list? — sailing is at the top."

"Aunt Mattie, you know how I feel about boats, but —" Julie bit her lip, and closed her eyes. She took a deep breath, held it for a minute, then faced the older woman and said, "Well, okay. I know there are lakes here around Phoenix, even if it is a desert. I suppose there's a small one with a sailboat somewhere close. That probably isn't really too dangerous. What else?"

"No, no, no. Not a lake. I said Robert Redford. Somewhere off Martha's Vineyard or Narraganset. Or . . . well, I don't know the names of those places. Cape Cod. That's it! Sailing with Robert Redford off Cape Cod."

"Mattie! That's ridiculous. Be serious now."

Mattie looked Julie straight in the eyes, and set her jaw firmly. "Well. You started this. Suddenly, I rather like the idea." She tilted her head. "Definitely sailing, though I might let you use a stand-in for Robert Redford. See who you can find. But no lake. It's got to be the New England seaboard." Mattie smiled, and reached out to take Julie's hand. "Now, honey, how many things can I have on this bucket list?"

"Uh . . . just one, I think."

And that's the way it all started.

"Edward, now what do I do? I've created a monster." Julie held the phone to her ear and pulled the blanket around her on the bed. "Aunt Mattie spent half the evening searching vacation home websites. She's determined to find a cottage on the seashore. On Cape Cod!"

Her husband chuckled on the other end of the line in Philadelphia. "I suppose you'd better start coordinating your vacation time with availability on the Cape. How soon does she want to go?"

"She's thinking of June, if she can find a rental. I don't know if I could get off work then or not." She slapped her hand against her forehead. "Oh, for heaven's sake, I sound as if I'm taking her seriously."

"Maybe you'd better take her seriously, sweetheart. She has a credit card. She knows how to book a plane ticket. She's perfectly capable of going without you. I'm not sure she could hook up with Robert Redford, but she could probably find a substitute."

"Oh, my God, what am I going to do? I wish you were here with me."

"Right now, I'm glad I'm not."

The coffee was ready, English muffins in the toaster, butter, jam, Greek yogurt and fresh peaches on the table when Julie came down the stairs in the morning. She hesitated before entering the room. Mattie stood beside the table, holding a cup of coffee with one hand, gazing out the patio door. Julie loved the way the turquoise pants suit she had sent for Mattie's seventieth birthday complemented her slim figure and grey hair. She knew the color would intensify the green of her aunt's eyes. Everything looked normal. Perhaps yesterday's conversation had been a bad dream. Julie stepped forward confidently.

"Good morning, Aunt Mattie. How are you? Breakfast looks yummy." She gave Mattie a warm hug, then smiled as she poured a cup of coffee and pushed the lever down on the toaster.

"I'm just great, honey. How are you? I haven't felt this good in a long time. I feel so alive this morning." Mattie turned back toward the patio and stretched her arms out in front of her. "There's a whole world out there I'd forgotten all about."

So the bad dream continues, Julie thought. "Yes, it is a wonderful world. I'm glad you're excited." Julie turned to the table and sat down. "But what about today? What time are we meeting Edna and Corinne for lunch?"

"Eleven o'clock, at the Blue Wildebeest. I'm so excited to tell them our plans. Corinne has been sailing before, but I wonder if Edna would come with us . . ."

Edna? Now Julie knew she was in trouble. Big trouble.

The Blue Wildebeest was Mattie's favorite restaurant, and she loved to take her guests there. Drumming African music engulfed them as she and Julie entered. A waiter dressed in zebra stripes led them along a path draped with mossy jungle vines hanging from tree branches above them. The distant howls and roars changed to chirping insect sounds and bird calls as they seemed to enter a dark, misty rainforest. They followed their guide on narrow wooden paths through a swamp where hooded eyes and silent ripples worried the ponds on either side.

Edna and Corinne had arrived first and were seated at the edge of what appeared to be the wide, grassy plains of the Serengeti. Realistic, moving projections of wildebeest, giraffe and antelope surrounded them.

"Julie, darling, how good to see you!" Edna stood up to greet them, no more self-conscious of her six-foot height than she had ever been. At age seventy her frame had not shrunk in the least, and her hair was almost as dark as Julie's.

Julie hugged her old friend, with just the slightest misgiving still in her thoughts. "Edna! I've missed you so much! Edward said to be sure and give you a hug from him. And Corinne, so good to see you. You're both looking great."

Corinne, shorter even than Mattie, and a bit rounder, stood up beside Edna and extended her arms. "Julie! Mattie's been looking forward to your visit, and so have we."

As they all sat down, Julie looked around the room. "I still can't understand how anyone would think of doing a restaurant like this when there's nothing outside but sand and rocks for hundreds of miles in any direction."

"That's why we love it! It's like taking a trip far away. I used to love to travel with Arthur. Did you know Art and I actually went to the Serengeti once, Julie?" asked Corinne.

Oh, no. Not Corinne too.

The Blue Wildebeest

"You'll never guess what Julie is going to do for me," Mattie said, sitting up straight with a smug look on her face. Clenching her fists, she leaned forward across the table toward her friends and whispered loudly. "She's going to take me sailing — on Cape Cod!"

"Julie! Mattie! How wonderful!" Edna clapped her hands together.

"We must have a glass of wine while you tell us all about it," said Corinne, and she jumped up, waving both hands to attract the waiter clothed in leopard spots. "How did you come up with this idea?"

"Julie asked me about my bucket list — you know — all the things you want to do that you haven't gotten to do yet, and . . ."

"Oh! I bet I have lots on my list if I think about it."

"Arthur just loved to go sailing, but we only did it a couple of times. When they unfurl the sail, it's just the most exciting thing!"

"Of course, you'll both come along, won't you?"

"There is so much history on Cape Cod. Whaling. Ship wrecks. Love stories."

"Martha's Vineyard."

"That's where they filmed *Jaws*."

"Nantucket Island."

"The Kennedy family and museum."

Julie slumped lower and lower into her chair as the three older women chattered and grew more and more excited.

There was no stopping them.

"Edward, how did I get myself into this?" Julie's eyes were red from crying, though her husband could only surmise that from the sniffling and panic he could hear in her voice. "She won't listen to reason, Edna and Corinne are practically packing their bags, and they're all arguing over what should be next on the bucket list!"

"Julie, Julie, Julie." Edward was used to having his wife bite off chunks that were too big for her to chew. Usually, he found it best to stand by and watch her work her own way through it. But this time, he was a little worried. He didn't want anything to hurt the deep, loving, protective relationship between Julie and her only living relative.

"I just can't stand the thought of her out on the ocean in a boat."

"Honey, just relax and maybe play along with them for a few days. They're having fun, but when it comes to taking concrete steps maybe they'll get tired of the game. Let them do a little dreaming."

"Dreaming, while I'm having a nightmare!" Julie twisted the corner of the sheet between her hands, as tears rolled down her cheek. "Boats sink, Edward! And I'm not sure she can even swim any more. She'd probably think a life jacket was silly."

"Julie, I know how you feel about boats, but cars and airplanes crash, too. That doesn't keep you from riding in them. And boats are probably the safest of the lot."

"My parents didn't die in a car or an airplane."

Chapter 2

When Julie was not quite six years old, her parents had taken a two-week escorted trip to Malaysia, leaving Julie to stay with Mattie while they were gone. When Mattie received word that the ferry carrying the tour group had capsized, she called Edna to come and be with her during the next agonizing hours and days, waiting for news. Tom and Meg were not among the survivors. Their bodies were never found. Julie had clung to Mattie day and night.

Mattie and Edna drove the grieving little girl back to Kansas City where the family had lived near Tom's elderly parents, the only other relatives. The family home had been left in Julie's name, with Mattie as the guardian and executor of the estate. While Mattie stayed in Kansas City with Julie, Edna returned to Phoenix. Together, she, Corinne, and Art had packed up the possessions Mattie wanted with her — personal items, plus the antiques and art decor that she had collected with her husband, Jake, before his death — rented a van and took them to her.

As Edna, Corrine and Art were busy moving Mattie's things into the house, Julie was playing in the back yard. She came in through the patio door just as Arthur was wrestling with a large painting of a sailboat, trying to lift it into position to hang above the couch in the living room. Julie stared at him for a moment, and was suddenly hysterical.

"Not that picture, Aunt Mattie! Please!" Julie had screamed, her whole body stiffening, fists clenched tight.

The four adults stared at her.

"What's wrong, honey?" Mattie had asked.

"It's a boat! It's a boat!" the child had sobbed, tears flooding down her frightened face. Years later, remembering, Julie could still feel the constriction in her chest, as she had begged them not to hang the picture.

After a moment, Mattie had understood and removed the painting from the wall. But she had not been willing to give it up completely, as Julie wanted her to. The offending painting was hung in the bedroom that had belonged to Julie's parents, and which would now be Mattie's. For all the years they shared the house, Julie avoided that room as much as possible.

Kansas City had been their home until Julie graduated from college, married Edward, and moved to Philadelphia. Soon after that, Mattie moved back to Phoenix, to the home she had kept, always thinking she would, one day, return. When Julie visited the first time, the painting had been the first thing she saw when she entered the house, in its old position over the fireplace. She had felt the tightening in her belly, then reminded herself that those were childish feelings. This was Mattie's house, and it was her picture. Julie had learned to accept, or ignore it. Until now.

As Julie hung up the phone, she let her thoughts drift back to those early memories. She didn't remember her parents clearly, though she remembered the fear and pain, and how lost she had felt. Mattie had been her rock, and Edna had been a constant presence during that first year as well.

Julie was just a toddler the first time she met Mattie's best friend. She had come with her parents (Mattie's sister, Meg, and brother-in-law, Tom) to visit from their home in Kansas City. Edna, invited to join them for lunch, burst into the room unexpectedly, her usual exuberant self. Julie had been shocked when Edna grabbed her up into her arms and hoisted her into the air, almost colliding with the ceiling. Julie had never met a woman so vivacious, so tall, so, frankly, terrifying. She had squealed and kicked, even as Edna returned her to the floor, then ran to Mattie's side and wrapped her arms around her legs, hiding her face.

"Oh, Julie, it's all right," soothed Mattie, leaning down to her, then turning to scold her friend. "Edna — you've frightened her to death! Haven't you learned to take it slow when meeting someone new, especially a child?"

"Oh, darling! I'm so sorry," said Edna. "Here — let me introduce myself properly." Edna lowered herself to her knees, and then sank down even lower, trying to make herself the same height as the frightened child.

"There, darling. Is that better? I am your Aunt Mattie's friend, Edna. You may call me Aunt Edna if you feel better that way, but just plain Edna is fine with me. I don't require any formalities. Your Aunt Mattie and I have been friends forever."

It was a rocky start, but by the end of the day, Julie and Edna had become fast friends as well.

Chapter 3

For three consecutive nights — evenings that Julie had thought to devote to going over old photos and memories — Edna, Corinne and Mattie hovered around the computer comparing one vacation rental with another, while Julie watched from the doorway. One too expensive, one just not picturesque enough, this one perfect, but too far from the waterfront.

"There has to be one that's just right!" said Corinne.

"Do you think we could ask your old travel agent, Corinne? Maybe she could find the right one."

"Oh, wait, look at this one! Julie! It even has a fireplace!" Julie moved closer, barely able to see between them. Mattie sat at the desk, with Edna and Corinne leaning over her. The computer screen showed a cottage surrounded by trees, the ocean clearly visible behind it, and a sheltered patio with Adirondack chairs and table.

"It's in our price range, and just a couple blocks from one of the marinas. There are three bedrooms, two with twin beds and one with a queen. Just darling! Edna and Corinne can have one room, you and Edward the master bedroom, and I'll take the little one. Unless, of course . . ." Mattie looked up, smiled coyly, and winked at Julie, ". . . unless Mr. Redford joins us."

Julie rolled her eyes and turned back into the other room without answering. She felt like a square peg in a round hole. Could these women she loved so much really be serious?

Safely out of earshot, she reached for her phone. "Edward, I really think they are going to make reservations. It's so expensive — they aren't rich women. I'll have to take off work to be with them."

"Julie, relax! Let them have their day in the sun. Sailing is not dangerous. There are all kinds of reputable sailing companies. Sign them up for a couple of tours. Send them whale watching. Just help them set it up, so you know they are dealing with good people. And we can spend at least the first couple of days with them."

"But Edward, they don't want my help. They don't listen to me. I feel like they don't even want me to hear their plans. Sometimes I think they're hiding something."

"Well, if you want them to start hiding their plans, just keep fussing at them, Julie. I think you've forgotten that this is the woman who raised you, the one who taught you to be strong, and independent. Mattie may be seventy, but she isn't senile or crippled. And if she needs bodyguards, you couldn't find anyone more dedicated to the task than Edna and Corinne. You are finding out right now just how formidable a trio they can be."

Julie had been in Arizona three days now, almost half of her planned week-long visit with Mattie. She had raised the idea of the bucket list on the day she arrived, with suggestions for vacations and shopping trips, but Mattie had smiled pleasantly and said, "But I really have everything I want right here, Julie. I have friends, a nice house, lots of books and flowers. Why would I want a bucket? When you and Edward are ready to have children, my life will be complete."

It wasn't until late that first evening that Mattie had been standing in the living room, looking at the painting of the sailboat hanging above the fireplace. She stood as if mesmerized and suddenly made that single-word statement that changed everything.

"Sailing."

What was it about that painting, Julie wondered? Why did Mattie love it so much?

Julie knew she had no right to resent Edna and Corinne for horning in on her plans with Mattie, but she couldn't seem to help herself. She'd had a picture of doing something special with Mattie, just the two of them, or maybe purchasing a special treasure that she would never get for herself. Surely there was something they could enjoy together. Now it just seemed to be a super production involving the three friends, not even needing Julie to help.

What did I expect her to ask for, Julie asked herself. A new car? She really does have everything she wants right here. Except a baby in the family. And I can't do anything about that right now. Julie squared her shoulders. I'm only thirty-five. I'll think about that later.

I just thought she might have some secret wish, and I could make her happy. Okay. So I found she does have a secret wish. But — sailing? Robert Redford? Cape Cod? And now it includes Edna and Corinne?

The idea felt dangerous to Julie. She pictured waves crashing against a rocky coast, a boat turned upside down, empty life vests floundering in the water. She shook the pictures from her mind, forced herself to think of Mattie instead. But then her head filled with all the sly, double meaning references to "Mr. Redford" or "Robert," as though she were a thirty-something looking for romance . . . Mattie wasn't rich, but some lecherous old man — or worse, a young one — could think she was rich long enough to cause her trouble. And she didn't seem to have a commercial tour boat in mind, but something more private, with just her and "Robert." It was so unlike the conventional, reserved, sensible woman who had raised her.

She chilled at the sudden thought that entered her mind: "Is this the way Alzheimer's starts?"

Chapter 4

Finally, on the fifth night of her visit, Julie and Mattie brought a stack of photo albums to the living room, along with a box of loose photos. A bottle of Merlot had accompanied their dinner, and they curled up on either end of the couch.

The first tattered album recorded the years Mattie and Edna had shared while in college where they had met. Shortly after graduation, the two of them had spent nearly a year in Europe, traveling by bicycle, sleeping in hostels.

"That was when you met Jake, wasn't it?" said Julie.

"Yes," said Mattie. Near the end of their trip, Mattie and Edna were caught in a sudden thunder storm. They took refuge in a small, French museum they would otherwise have missed. Jake, an attractive, athletic artist studying his way through all the famous museums of Europe, had joined them.

"I've loved rainstorms since that day," said Mattie. "Without it, Jake and I might never have met. Before the storm was over we knew we were meant to be together." Edna returned home as planned, but Mattie stayed in Europe, traveling with Jake while he studied the masters and practiced his own artistic skills. Returning to the states, they married and settled in Phoenix.

Edna had spent a few seasons pursuing a career on the stage, with a bit of success. Julie knew Edna had left the stage after falling in love, but didn't know how it had ended. Mattie had tended to be somewhat guarded about details of their past, but recently had begun to share more. After all, Julie was all grown up now, even though Mattie sometimes seemed reluctant to recognize that.

"So how did you meet Corinne and Arthur?" Julie asked, as she picked up an old photo, showing the two couples together. "Were they in college with you, too?"

"No. We were living in Phoenix when we met them. We don't often talk about how we met, because it has to include Edna's story," Mattie said.

"Edna's story? But you knew Edna long before that."

Mattie picked up another photo. A young, vibrant looking Edna stood a bit taller than the dark, handsome young man in uniform. They gazed at each other with obvious infatuation.

"Edna always fell in love easily, but with Steven she was completely swept off her feet. For him, she forgot all her aspirations about the stage. She was touring with an off-Broadway production when she met him. He was in the Marines, and she moved in with him in the middle of a production, pretty much ending her hopes of a career on stage."

"I remember her mentioning Steven now and then," said Julie, "though I never knew he was more special than some of her other beaus."

"They were together a little over a year when he was sent to Vietnam. They had just found out that Edna was pregnant." Mattie took a deep breath. "He never came back. It was officially "Missing in Action" for about three years before they found his remains, but they knew the helicopter had crashed in flames and that there were no survivors."

Mattie paused, and Julie touched her hand softly.

"Edna had a baby? I never heard that."

"That was what held her together when Steven died. She came here and stayed with Jake and me for a few months. She kept saying 'At least I'll have his child.' A few weeks before the baby was due, she found a condo to buy, moved in and fixed up a nursery. She seemed happy for the first time since losing Steven."

Mattie stared at the photo in her hands. "The baby struggled to live for several hours after a difficult labor and birth. Edna was devastated when the little boy died in her arms. She curled up in her apartment, staring at the TV. She must have eaten something, but I don't know what. I saw a frozen pizza box now and then. Always a bottle of wine beside her. Jake and I tried to get her to come stay with us, but she wouldn't. We took her meals, but I never saw her eat them. After a while, she barely answered the door and wouldn't let us in. It was like we were part of the past she would not accept. She's never been able to talk about it. At the time, she completely fell apart."

"How awful for Edna," whispered Julie.

Mattie reached out to take Julie's hand, blinked back tears, and continued. "One night she went out to get more wine. Returning home, she stumbled on the steps to her apartment and dropped the bag holding the bottles. The cuts were not deep, thankfully, but they bled heavily. Especially the one on her scalp. It was Arthur, who lived in the neighboring unit, who found her on the steps, unconscious and bleeding, when he came home from an evening meeting. At first he thought he'd stumbled onto a murder scene and he shouted for Corrine to call 911.

"By the time the ambulance arrived, they could see the wounds were not life threatening. They went with her to the ER, but she refused to be admitted. Arthur and Corinne, complete strangers to her the day before, took her to their own home and began to care for her as if she were a child. For the first week, one of them was by her side night and day. They fed her soups, and then a hearty stew, sandwiches, all the things she had refused from Jake and me. Somehow, they were able to get through to her. For Corinne and Art, it was a place to focus all their need to nurture, and slowly Edna recovered and learned to live again."

"Wow," said Julie quietly. "I had no idea."

"Corinne and Arthur had lost two babies, one in early pregnancy, one nearly full term. They felt Edna's loss as if it were their own. The three of them became almost inseparable. Two years after meeting Edna, Corinne learned that she would have to have a hysterectomy, ending once and for all their hope of having a child of their own. Then it was Corinne's turn to lean on Edna."

"No wonder Edna and Corinne are so close."

"By that time, Jake was losing ground, and we knew our time was limited," Mattie continued. "The three of them were my support while he faded away over the next four years."

"You've been through so much together. You really are like family to each other," said Julie.

Mattie reached over and hugged Julie. "Two years after Jake died, we got the message that your parents had been lost. Edna, Corinne and Arthur wanted me to stay in Phoenix, and raise you here, but I thought it would be better to be close to your father's parents. I think it was the right decision. You needed them, and they needed you to be with them. And I needed them to share decisions for you. It was such a painful time for all of us."

Silently, Julie filled their wine glasses. Then she reached for another album. A young couple holding a newborn baby smiled from a photo on the front cover. Julie caressed the photo tenderly. "Mommy was beautiful, wasn't she? She looked a lot like you, Aunt Mattie." Her voice was soft. "I'm glad we lived close to Grandma and Grandpa. They were the only ones who ever talked about Mommy and Daddy. They were part of those early years, and they used to tell me stories about when I was a baby, and things Mommy and Daddy did. They kept some memories alive. After they died, everything seemed to fade away."

"I'm sorry, Julie. I had no idea how to help you. I didn't want to remind you. I know now that was wrong. Thank goodness they were there for you."

"I didn't mean that the way it sounded. You were there for me too, Mattie. You were always there. We had each other."

"We still have each other, Julie. Thank goodness."

"I understood why you wanted to return here after I got married and moved away," said Julie. "I'm so glad you have your own special family. But, Mattie, I'm afraid for you. You aren't young any more. The world isn't like it was when you and Edna bicycled all over Europe. Corinne seems so innocently naive, and you seem so — so — well, vulnerable." She gritted her jaw and spat out the words. "And just plain silly, Aunt Mattie! Do you really think you are going to find a Robert Redford out there?"

"Julie, isn't it okay to pretend a bit? Of course I don't expect to find a Robert Redford. But that doesn't mean I can't experience something new and different, does it?"

"I really wish I'd never brought it up," whined Julie. "I just can't bear to think of you out on a boat. In the ocean. What in the world made you pick sailing? I'm terrified, Aunt Mattie. I keep seeing you floundering in monstrous waves beside an overturned boat." She covered her face with her hands.

"Darling. I know how you feel about boats, although I didn't even think of that when the idea popped into my head. But, Julie, you can't let it rule your life." She gently touched Julie's chin and looked straight into her eyes. "Or mine."

"It's that picture, isn't it?" Julie waved her hand toward the fireplace. "The one I didn't want you to bring to Kansas City. I'd forgotten how upset it made me. I wouldn't let you hang it in the living room, but you hung it in your bedroom. Why does it mean so much to you?"

It was a magical painting for Mattie, from the first moment she saw it. Not especially happy, but magical. It hung in a small gallery on the coast near Carmel-by-the-Sea. Maybe it was the enchantment of the day as she and Jake wandered the village that was Carmel in the late '60s.

They were staying in a cottage just steps from the white sands of the beach stretching toward the incredibly blue water.

"When you don't have much time, you have to use it wisely," Jake said, as they considered whether to take a whale boat ride or simply explore the beach and shops that final afternoon of their stay.

She knew he was referring to the reservation taking them back to Phoenix the next day. She knew he didn't mean the "year — maybe two" the doctors had predicted on their last visit to the clinic. But that's the way she interpreted it in her heart. She could see whales some other time. What she wanted today was to capture all the togetherness — all the Jake-ness — she could possibly crowd into the days and hours she had left with him.

So, they strolled the boardwalk, going into all of the art galleries, searching for just the right choice of souvenir to take back to their home with them. The painting wasn't in the window. It was toward the back of the store, set between ropes and nets, buoys and starfish, decorating the wall.

It wasn't the sailboat that first caught her eye. It was the figure of the man sitting at the end of the pier, looking out over the water at the sailboat that was coming toward him.

In the foreground, there were flowers, a chair, the trunk of a tree, and flagstones, as if seen from the patio of a cottage. A short distance away was the entrance to a fishing pier that stretched out into the ocean. At the end of the pier, a man in a drab blue coat faced out to sea, with his back toward the cottage, and beyond him, a sail boat with a red half-sail rose on a wave, like a soaring white bird returning to shore.

Then, inexplicably, the perspective changed for her, and it seemed the boat was not coming toward the pier, but going out toward the sea, away from the shore. For a moment, she thought the man was on the boat, then she blinked her eyes and saw that the figure still sat on the edge of the pier, waiting — for what?

She walked up closer to the picture, reached up and touched it. Jake was beside her.

"It's perfect for above the fireplace, isn't it?" he said.

"Yes. But why? A seascape in the middle of the Arizona desert? It's sort of incongruous, don't you think?"

"Yes, but somehow, it fits."

"I didn't know . . . that it was from your time with Jake. You were happy together, Mattie. Why didn't you and Jake have a baby of your own?"

Mattie looked away. "I was afraid, I guess. I knew I'd be raising the child alone. Silly, wasn't I? If I hadn't had you to raise, I don't know what I would have done with myself."

"I wanted to do something special for you," said Julie. "I thought there would be something you and I could do together, or something I could buy for you. I never dreamed you'd want to do something dangerous, or take off across the country with two other old ladies like yourself who haven't been outside Phoenix for fifteen years."

"Julie. Did you really want to do something special for me?"

"Yes, Mattie — I really did. I really do. Because I love you. But..."

"Well, Julie, you have." Mattie put her hands on Julie's shoulders. "This is special. Not just a one moment special, but a rest-of-my-life special. Can you see the difference? I was just sitting here waiting to get old. Waiting for you to have a baby. Oh, I still want that to happen soon, but now, all of a sudden, I feel like I'm getting younger every day. Julie, I'm looking forward to next summer. I'm making plans, instead of walking around in memories. Memories are nice, I wouldn't give them up for the world, but I want to make new memories for as long as I can." She searched for the right words. "And you have made me see that I can still make memories. Just planning this is making my life so much richer. You've done something so much more special than you ever imagined."

"Oh, Mattie. I love you so much. Okay. I'll try and help you with this." Julie took a deep breath and straightened her shoulders. "Boat or no boat."

"That's my girl." Mattie gave her a hug, told her goodnight and went upstairs to her bedroom.

Mattie stretched out on the bed, closed her eyes and let herself float back in time. Jake had been strong and healthy when they met, and for the early part of their marriage they had hiked, skied, even spent part of one summer backpacking the Adirondacks. A talented artist, he earned good commissions as a graphic design artist for a major company in Phoenix, but she loved to watch him coax color and shapes into the landscapes he sold along the way when they traveled, to help pay their expenses.

She remembered the first day that he lagged behind her on a relatively easy day hike. He had blamed it on not getting enough sleep the night before, but Mattie could tell he was puzzled. The hikes had been getting more difficult for him, though she didn't seem to be bothered by them. He tried lifting weights, but found he just got weaker. Then the day came when he was barely able to finish a trail they had hiked easily many times. Frightened, when they reached the car Mattie got behind the wheel and drove them directly to an emergency room. After weeks of testing, Jake was diagnosed with a rare form of muscular dystrophy. Treatments available at the time could not stop the steady progression of the degenerative disease.

Forced to give up their active schedule, he concentrated on his art work, thankful he was able to continue to make a good income, and he made careful investments to provide a comfortable living for Mattie when he was gone. Eventually they found the bad days outnumbering the good days, and slowly he slipped further and further away from her. With help from Edna and Corinne, she was able to care for him at home, and it was here, in this very room, that he smiled his last weak smile and whispered goodbye.

Chapter 5

Julie sifted through the loose photos, bringing a flood of her own memories — memory after memory. Photos of Julie with Mattie in Kansas City, as well as together in Phoenix. Almost as many of Julie with Edna. Often, she had spent vacations with Edna, relishing the excitement and freedom it provided. Mattie, as a single parent, tended to be too restrictive, while Edna knew no fear.

Here was an album of the summer Julie was nine years old and had spent a month with Edna while Mattie was away at summer school. They had gone to art galleries, museums, concerts, dinner at a dozen different restaurants, the zoo, the amusement park, even on a hot air balloon ride, and Edna had spent a small fortune purchasing a trunk full of souvenirs for Julie to take home with her.

"Were you friends with Aunt Mattie when you were little girls?" Julie had asked as they sat on the patio one evening waiting for a pizza to be delivered. (After all, Julie was nine years old. Fancy restaurants weren't the only way to eat.)

"No," answered Edna. "We met as roommates when we started college. We were both eighteen years old. Mattie had been raised in a very small town, and everything was new and confusing to her — the traffic, using a bus to get around, scheduling classes, finding her way around in strange places, and meeting new people every day."

"I thought Aunt Mattie always knew everything. Mommy used to say that Mattie was the smartest person in the whole family. She's always been a teacher, hasn't she?"

"Not before she went to college, sweetheart! You have to grow up and get training before you start on your career, especially teaching."

"But you knew everything already?"

"No, of course not. In lots of ways, I didn't know as much as Mattie. But I did know about the city, and crowds and waiting in line and how to navigate different offices and red tape, I guess I was better at that, and I could help Mattie with those things."

"But she knew some things better?"

"Yes, Julie. Mattie was wiser than I in many ways. She was cautious, thoughtful, and she had a better understanding of people. She kept me out of trouble more than once."

"Trouble?"

"Well, some stories better wait until you are older. Look, here comes the pizza."

When Julie was seventeen, the summer before her senior year in high school, Edna and Mattie together took her to Hawaii for ten days. They snorkeled, tried surfing, climbed a volcano, learned the hula, and ate so many exotic dishes that Julie thought she would never be satisfied with barbequed ribs again. They were close, the three of them, but it was always Edna who planned the itinerary, and pooh-poohed Mattie's caution. Mattie constantly warned Julie to be careful, and tried to hold her back. Julie had swallowed her fears and let Edna scare her, amaze her and delight her.

Now, as she looked through the photos, Julie realized how their roles had turned, with Julie now worried about keeping Mattie safe. But Julie knew Edna could throw caution to the wind, and while that had been acceptable for herself when she was eighteen, Julie did not want her beloved Mattie to be exposed to any danger. Mattie, to her, had always been tame, cautious, even frightened of adventure. Julie didn't think Mattie would know how to handle new situations.

If Edna was the flamboyant "Auntie Mame," always ready for new experiences, Corinne could almost have played the role of Grandma during those years, with her quiet, matronly manner. Julie had not realized she could be completely different, and she often thought of Corinne as being older than Mattie and Edna. Of course, she was usually with Arthur, until five years before when he had died suddenly of a heart attack. She, Edna, and Mattie had been inseparable after that.

But they never seemed to do much. They played bridge monthly at the club they belonged to, met for lunch at least once a week, attended an occasional concert or play, and seemed content with their low-key lives. Julie had only thought to offer Mattie a small sparkle of difference, not necessarily excitement.

She did love Mattie's friends. They were family to each other. Next to herself, Julie knew Mattie loved Corinne and Edna more than anyone.

Chapter 6

"What a gorgeous sunrise!" exclaimed Julie. She opened the door for Mattie and they both stepped out onto the patio, coffee in hand. The sky glowed with streaks of reds and golds. "It's been wonderful to enjoy this every morning. If Edward and I had a view like this from our apartment in Philadelphia, getting up early would be easier."

Mattie agreed, as she pulled a chair closer to the table and sat down. "A cup of good coffee and a sky like this, with the birds singing all around us — it's a great way to start any day."

Julie stood quietly for a moment before sitting down. Her suitcase was packed, and she had called a taxi to pick her up in an hour. "It's been a wonderful week, in spite of all the craziness, Aunt Mattie. I guess a week on Cape Cod is not unreasonable. But promise me you won't get on a sailboat without Edward and me there."

"You're such a worrier, Julie. If I'd been as protective of you while you were growing up, you'd have rebelled and run away with the circus. Edna and Corinne and I will be fine. We'll watch out for each other."

"That's not very comforting, Mattie."

"And you and Edward can spend as much time with us as you are able to get away from work. I know summers are busy with tourists in Philadelphia, but we can't very well sail in the winter. At least not comfortably."

"Mattie, you know I want you to be happy. But safe, too. I wouldn't know what to do without you."

"Someday, Julie, you know, you will have to learn to make a life without me. Life doesn't stay the same forever, never changing."

"Mattie. You are all I've ever had."

"Not true! You have Edward, and one day, God willing, a child. Take it from me, Julie. A child is a blessing. And, Julie, you had a mother and father to whom you were the whole world."

"I wonder what would have happened to me without you, Mattie."

They hugged each other warmly. "You need to have some faith in my common sense, Julie. I won't be reckless. At least not nearly as much as I might have been in years past. But it does feel good to be excited about the future." The color disappeared from the sky as the sun popped over the horizon. "So what would you put on your bucket list, Julie?" Mattie turned toward her. "What are the unfulfilled dreams in your life?"

"There's still so much time for me. Sometimes it seems like too much time. I don't know what I will do with it." Julie swirled her cup. "Edward wants to have a baby. But I'm not in a hurry. Of course we'll have a baby someday. Now, hearing about Edna's loss, and Corinne's, it is even more scary. And babies take so much time and money."

Mattie smiled. They'd had this conversation before.

"What is it you're so afraid of, Julie? You and Edward will be wonderful parents."

Julie ignored the question.

"Have fun with your wacky plans, Mattie. Edward tells me that I'm silly to worry about you three. I do feel okay about your trip now. I just hope it won't be too adventurous. And Edward and I will be there to meet you and help you get settled in. Remember the time we rented that condo in San Diego and it turned out to have fifty-three stairs we had to climb to get to our room? No elevator! And that was before we learned to pack light!"

"Julie, I will always be glad you suggested the bucket list — although I don't think of it as a bucket list anymore — just a new way of living the rest of my life. Start yours soon, Julie. Don't be afraid to take risks."

Chapter 7

The weeks spun by faster than Mattie could remember them doing in a long time. She spent hours with Edna and Corinne web-surfing to find out all they could about the Cape Cod area, from artsy Provincetown to marine research in Woods Hole. There were day-long sailing excursions offered, evening sunset cruises, two-hour tours of the bay, and even private sailing lessons.

They learned about shipwrecks and stories of lost loves. "We'd better not tell Julie about those."

"Whale hunting was the main industry for centuries. How awful! But now we can go whale watching. I hope we get to see one up close."

"Look, this is where they made Sandwich Glass. Julie has a dozen antique pieces that her mother collected. There's just a museum now, but I'll bet that's something Julie would like to see."

"My old travel agent says that most people fly into Boston or Providence and rent a car, or take a shuttle, which takes about two hours," said Corinne. "Does anyone want to drive that far on unfamiliar roads?" All three shook their heads.

"If Julie and Edward come at the same time, we could share a car," said Mattie, "but they haven't gotten their vacation time confirmed yet. I guess I'd rather not have to depend on meeting up with them, so let's book the shuttle."

The travel agent recommended a tiny village tucked away on the mid-cape, sheltered from the Atlantic in a small cove. Shelton was as quiet as any place on the Cape could hope to be, she said, and still offered easy access to other areas. It had a small beach close to rental cottages, a marina and easy walking around the shops and town square. She steered them to a website where they could look over cottages available.

There was so much they wanted to see and do. They read about restaurants, special historical sites, and even homes of celebrities. "Doesn't look like Robert Redford frequents the area, but oh, well!"

Soon they began planning their wardrobes. Corinne led them to her favorite stores. "Remember, we might get splashed, so nothing that is going to fade down our legs, or onto the rest of our clothing. Light-weight fabrics that will roll up tight in the suitcase and shake out wrinkle-free. We don't want anything to shrink up and leave our boobs exposed. No one is going to be too excited about seeing them!"

Sandals seemed right to Mattie, picking up a sporty wedge, but Corinne insisted on canvas deck shoes. "You don't want to be slipping and sliding overboard."

"Jeans and shorts?" asked Edna.

Corinne shook her head. "For us, I think capri-length pants. Tanks and sleeveless tops will do. As long as you choose a matching cover-up."

Mattie and Edna deferred to Corinne's guidelines for the most part, moving from department to department on their third shopping trip. It was the first time she actually let them make some purchases.

"We need to look at everything, get a feel for what is in style for the season, the colors, fabrics, and all that. You don't want to spend a bunch of money, then start seeing things you like so much better."

They finished the afternoon with dinner at the Wildebeest.

"How is Julie doing?" asked Edna.

"She's still nervous, I can tell, so I give her enough information to make her happy and feel included. She's really glad we are going through your travel agent instead of booking things ourselves. She still wants to check out the rental agency, and all the tour operators, so that keeps her busy."

"She's learning what it's like to be a mother, I suspect. A mother to three old ladies."

"Don't use the "O" word," scolded Edna. They laughed. "Sometimes, I think Julie's older than any of us."

Mattie pulled a journal from her bag, and opened it. "So — are we all in? Cost for the bungalow, flight and the shuttle are nearly firmed up. Groceries will come to about what we would spend right here at home. Plus eating out, fun, excursions, souvenirs. Even if there are unexpected problems, we can swing it, right?"

Edna nodded. "None of us has a whole lot of money, but we each have some, and we might as well spend it. I've been saying that for years, but didn't know what to spend it on besides eating out, having my hair done and my massage therapist. Mattie, you've lightened up the world."

A huge grin broke over Corinne's face. "I thought my traveling days were over," she said. "I just sat back and stopped dreaming after Arthur died. If I hadn't had you two to have lunch with and a glass of wine now and then, I'd probably have died too. Why didn't we think of this before?"

"It's amazing, isn't it?" Edna said. "Somehow, we let ourselves think that once we were alone and over the age of 60, we should just be content with what we'd already done. And we were. At least I was. Were you feeling unhappy, cheated, at all?" Edna looked at her two friends.

"Not a bit," answered Mattie. "And it didn't happen all at once. I just sort of drifted into a routine of reading books, going to the pool for exercise, talking to Julie on the phone, lunches here at The Blue Wildebeest whenever there was someone to come with. Sometimes I even came here alone. I didn't realize it, but I guess it was the outrageousness of the decor that made it so much fun to come here. It just seemed a little out of the ordinary, but it was enough. I wasn't feeling the need for anything more exciting."

Chapter 8

After they decided on a rental cottage, they made a final visit to the travel agent. She confirmed the plane reservations, scheduled the shuttle to and from their cottage, and gave them each a sheaf of brochures and a guide book, along with the itinerary. For the first time in weeks, nothing demanded attention or decision-making at the moment. They relaxed with a pot of coffee on Mattie's patio.

"So — what's on your bucket list, Edna? Corinne?"

Edna lifted her coffee cup but did not drink from it. Instead, she swirled it slightly, like a cup of tea, as if she were trying to read her fortune there. "I've been thinking about that. I spent enough time on the stage to have satisfied that childhood dream. Having a child has been on the 'never-happened' list for longer that it was on 'the maybe some-day' list. I've been to Paris and Rome, seen the Pieta, walked along the Seine. How did you come up with sailing, Mattie? You never mentioned it. It would have been easy enough to do when we were younger."

"I don't really know." Mattie pointed inside, through the patio door. "It was like the picture suddenly came to life. The sailboat was calling to me. Silly. When Jake and I found the painting, we already knew he was dying, but there were still a few fairly good months left to us."

For a moment, Mattie could hear Jake's voice.

"I don't want you to spend your life alone, Mattie. Much as I wish it could be you and I together for the next 50 years."

"Don't talk about that, Jake. I can't bear to think of living without you, and thinking of someone else is — well, even more unthinkable."

"I'll send someone for you," he said. "I'll send someone in that sailboat. You'll know it when you see the red half-sail. When you see it swinging around and heading in, you will know." He was smiling.

She had laughed, bitterly. "When I see a sailboat coming in over the sand, I'll remember your promise."

Mattie had forgotten the conversation, but it came back to her now. Julie had been the wind in her sails for fifteen years. Her ship had been becalmed for ten. And now, she saw the red half-sail turning toward her.

"Somehow, that painting has signified those few wonderful years I shared with Jake, as well as him slowly sailing out of my life." Mattie shrugged her shoulders and smiled wistfully. "I want to get on that sailboat and dream for a while about being in love again."

Edna set the cup and saucer back down on the table.

"Memories. What would we do without them?"

"Memories are great," agreed Corinne. "But, back to the bucket list."

"Everything on mine passed by unclaimed many years ago."

"No, Edna. We aren't talking about the past," said Corinne. "This is about the next twenty years. I mean, we could easily have that many, even more. Are we going to practice rocking all that time?"

"You're right," said Mattie. "We've sort of gotten in a rut, haven't we?" They were silent for a few minutes.

"Rafting the Grand Canyon," Edna said quietly. "I know that's from the past. Steven and I were going to do that for our honeymoon. But you know, I never really stopped imagining what it would be like. I've seen it from the top, both rims, but I've heard it's even more exciting — amazing — from the river."

"Art and I were trying to arrange a trip on the Yangtze. He wanted to get there before it was dammed."

They all sat quietly for a minute.

"A few nights before Jake died, just as he was falling asleep, he smiled at me and whispered 'Don't wait too long. I'll send a sail boat for you.' I thought he meant when it was time for me to follow him. But now I wonder." She indicated the painting. "I used to think the boat was coming to get him and take him away from me. That may have been right once, but it doesn't seem right any more. It used to be lonely, sad. Now it seems happy, adventurous, an invitation."

After a moment, Corinne sat up straighter, and looked back and forth at her friends.

"Well, what else? If we've got twenty years — or for that matter ten, or five or even... Is there something we're forgetting to do?"

"I'd like to swim in the ocean again," offered Edna.

"We can take care of that one easily on Cape Cod."

"Corinne, can we check one off for you while we're there?" asked Mattie.

"Climb up in a lighthouse. Don't know why Art and I never did that. We had lots of opportunities. They must have a lighthouse on Cape Cod."

"I've never ridden on a motorcycle. Never thought about it, really. But it might be pretty exciting." Mattie grinned.

"Steven rode a Harley, and I went with him a few times. It was exciting. I told him once it must be like driving a team of horses. Now, that might be fun to do."

"Hang gliding! I once told Jake I wanted to try that when I got too old to be afraid. I'm not sure I'm old enough yet. But someday, soon."

"Would you be shocked if I said I'd like to try marijuana?" said Corinne. "Just once. But I'd have to be sure I wouldn't get caught. I'd hate to go to jail. I guess we could go to Colorado."

Mattie looked at Edna, wide eyed. "Psychedelic mushrooms. That was my secret desire years ago. But raising Julie, I couldn't do dangerous or illegal stuff."

"Speaking of Julie," said Corinne, "I don't think she'd approve of many of our choices so far."

Mattie nodded her head. "To find a way to help Julie not be so afraid. I failed that one over the years. That should probably be number one on my bucket list."

"I think what she was hoping for were things you and she could do together. When she was a little girl, she used to follow all the horses in the Kentucky Derby leading up to the race. Remember how we would all get together to watch the race on TV? Do you think she'd still like to go to it . . . for real?"

"That's a good idea, Edna. I wonder how we could get tickets."

"What about a Broadway play? I know you've done that, Edna. I'll bet Julie would love to go to one."

Mattie's eyes began to get misty. "More than anything in the world, I'd like to experience a total solar eclipse — one where it actually gets dark and the animals go to roost."

"Then there are all the naughty things we would never have thought about years ago. A day at a nudist colony."

"Sneaking into a movie."

"Wearing a bikini. Topless."

"Paper and pen. Let's make a list. We don't need to do all of them, but let's choose at least one every year and just do it!"

"We can add to it whenever we think of something else."

"Julie will just die if she ever sees it."

"If? We are going to send her a copy!"

PART TWO
CAPE COD

Chapter 9

Mattie, Corinne, and Edna made their way through the crowded Boston airport until they found the luggage carousel and claimed their bags. One apiece, plus their carry-ons. They stepped to the side, out of the crowd and looked around. Julie and Edward were supposed to arrive an hour earlier, but there was no sign of them. Where were they? Just as they headed for the passenger pick-up area, Mattie's cell phone rang.

Julie sounded frantic. "Our flight was diverted! We're stuck in Newark. I don't know when we will get there."

"Newark? Didn't know you went through there."

"We weren't supposed to. They are checking the engines or something. I'm just worried about you."

"It's okay, Julie. We'll be fine. The shuttle will take us to the Cape and you can just meet us there."

"But what if it isn't like it's supposed to be? What if the house isn't available when you get there? What if it turns out to be a dump? Listen Mattie, just get a motel room close to the airport where you are and wait for us there."

"Oh, for heaven's sake, Julie! You'd think none of us had ever been outside Podunk Center before! Just call us when you know you're on the way. Oh! There's our shuttle. 'Bye now!"

She slipped her cell phone into her purse, and chuckled. "Julie and Edward are stuck in Newark. She wants us to get a motel here and wait for them! Come on, let's get on that shuttle."

"She hung up on me!" Julie clutched Edward's arm. "What do we do?"

He put his arm around her shoulders, shook his head, and sighed audibly. "We calm down and get a sandwich while we're stuck here. I'm just glad they let us off the plane and didn't keep us sitting on the tarmac. Really, I'm more concerned about how long we might have to stay here than about Mattie and her friends. Relax, Julie. They can take care of themselves." He steered her toward the closest sandwich shop.

"I'm sure they can," Julie said. "But I'd feel better if they waited for us in Boston."

"Why would that be any better? Suppose we don't get out of Newark for hours? The shuttle is there to pick them up, and they might as well be getting settled. We'll rent a car when we get to Boston and cancel the one we had reserved on the Cape."

"You're right, of course." She smiled at him. "You're always right, Edward. I'm really trying to relax. I want to enjoy this week."

"My name's Charlie," said the burley, six-foot, two-hundred-fifty-pound driver, as he hefted their bags into the back of the van. "You're my only passengers today. It's nice to have three of you. Sometimes it's just one. Shelton is pretty small, but sometimes I pick up folks going to the other areas."

"Our travel agent recommended Shelton to us. She's had several other clients stay there, and they all loved it," said Corinne.

"You'll love it too," he said.

Charlie pointed out points of interest while in the Boston area, but the long flight from Phoenix had tired them, and all three dozed off and on during the two-hour ride south. As they neared the Bourne Bridge which would take them onto Cape Cod, Charlie asked if they were awake.

"The view is spectacular from here. You won't want to miss this," he said. "That is, unless heights and insane traffic scare you, in which case, close your eyes, and find something to bury your head in. Once we cross the bridge, you are officially on Cape Cod."

"Wow, what a beautiful bridge!" said Edna. "And what a span over that river." A graceful bridge arched across a wide, straight body of water, beyond which were green, rolling hills.

"I didn't know there was a river here," said Corinne.

"It's not a river," explained Charlie. "It's a canal that was cut from the Atlantic north to the bay. Opened in 1911 with a draw bridge. This arch bridge replaced it in 1935. The canal actually makes the Cape an island. Before that, it was a long sail up around Provincetown and down the outer coast. And it was dangerous. Now barges go easily across the canal. There are two bridges, and you have to cross one of them to get onto the Cape. Both are traffic nightmares."

After crossing the bridge, Charlie stayed on the highway as they traveled past signs to villages on either side. "You'll want to explore some of these towns, but for now, I think you are probably anxious to get to your place and get settled before nightfall."

"You're right," said Mattie. "It has been a long day. But I can't wait to have a look around the town."

Finally, they saw the sign that said Shelton, and Charlie turned off the main highway. They wound through woods, meadows and low hills for a few miles, before they came around a curve in the road, and the women gasped. In front of them, blue water stretched across a sheltered cove. To the right the water extended toward the open sea, while across the water in front of them dark forests lined the shore. Sandy beaches could be seen along the cove to the left.

"If the cove were bigger, we'd probably have a lot more visitors," said Charlie. "But we don't have any motels, and not a whole lot of rentals either. The beaches are small, and there are just a few shops and restaurants. We're still busy, as every place on the Cape is, but this is quieter than most. We have a festival in a couple of weeks and we get real crowded that weekend. Will you be staying that long?"

"Only a week," said Edna. "I think we have you booked to take us back to Boston a week from today. This looks like a place I could stay for a month."

Nearing the cove, the road branched with one fork going each direction. Charlie turned to the right and drove along the waterfront, past houses and meadows. He stopped so they could look out over the water, showing them where they could get down to a beach. Returning to where the road branched, they went the other direction, which led to a small town.

"The town has everything you need," he said as they entered the village, "but not a whole lot more. Population's about 3500."

Along the waterfront was a marina, a fishing pier and a cluster of shops. Houses lined the road on the other side for several blocks, and spilled inland, stretching into the trees. Charlie turned up one street, and after going just half a block, stopped in front of a quaint cottage, the water just across the road, the marina and the fishing dock in sight.

"Here's your address, ladies. It's a perfect location you chose," he said. "I'll help you with your bags, and make sure the key is where it's supposed to be. This outfit you rented from does a real good job of making sure everything is ready for you, but now and then there's a glitch with the key or something. They'll take care of anything that isn't right," said Charlie.

Corinne was the first to speak as they got out of the van and looked at what would be their home for the next week. "It's perfect!" she breathed.

"Just like the pictures," crooned Edna." And you can just taste the salt and ocean in the air."

"At least on the outside," said Mattie, having been at least slightly influenced by Julie's skepticism. She used the code she had been given by the rental agency to get the key from the lockbox and stepped to the front door. The key turned easily and the door swung open.

They stepped into a bright, cheery living room. A picture window next to the door framed a lovely view of the waterfront and the water beyond. A fireplace, with kindling and logs stacked to the side, was centered on the left wall. To the right a door opened to a warm kitchen, while another led into a room lined with windows and bookshelves. It looked as though the owners had just stepped out to the store.

"Looks like everything is in order," said Charlie, handing them a card. "I have a local cab service along with the shuttle. Just me and my wife. If you need transportation anywhere, just call. I'll be running along now. Maybe we'll run into you later in the week, downtown or on the beach. Have a great vacation, ladies."

They thanked him profusely and Mattie tucked a generous tip in his hand. She closed the door behind him and ran to join the other two who were already exploring the bedrooms and inspecting the kitchen.

"I feel just like a kid on Christmas morning," cried Corinne, spinning around in the center of the bedroom before flopping down in the middle of the bed on her back. "What shall we do first?"

"Unpack," answered Edna. "I won't want to do it later."

Soon they were putting empty suitcases into the back of the closet, and tucking toiletries into the shelves and drawers.

"We'll be here a week, and I want to be comfortable," said Mattie.

They gathered in the kitchen when they finished and explored the cupboards there. Plenty of dishes, pans, silverware and linens.

"I suppose the first thing on the agenda might be laying in some groceries," said Corinne. "I'm hungry already."

"We can eat out tonight, but we'd better have something for morning, at least," agreed Mattie.

They each brushed their hair, freshened lipstick, slipped on a light sweater, and together they stepped out the door into their adventure. Across the road in front of them, a wooden walkway led along the edge of the road toward the cluster of shops they had passed before.

Charlie had told them they could find groceries just past the fishing pier. "Not a supermarket," he said, "but you'll find the basics there. And he keeps the place open until ten o'clock."

They strolled down the walk at a leisurely pace, the sound of the waves providing a background to their friendly chatter.

"It's just like it's supposed to be," cried Mattie.

"I haven't felt like a tourist for years," exclaimed Corinne. "And I loved being a tourist, even if we didn't spend much money. Art always said I was the happiest tourist he knew, but if the locals had to depend on me for their support, they'd soon be out of business."

"The best places to be a tourist are in the places the tourists haven't found yet," declared Edna. "But this is delightful. Let's go down and look at the boats. I think one of the rental places we liked on the computer was at this marina."

They moved on down the pathway, and in minutes had reached the shops, and paused to look in the windows.

"Let's walk out on the pier," suggested Corinne, pointing ahead. A bait shop marked the entrance to the fishing pier which stretched out into the water.

Reaching it, they turned and started down the pier, Mattie leading the way. Suddenly, she lifted her arms out to the side, stopping her friends.

"Look," she said, staring ahead of them.

Edna gasped.

"What?" asked Corinne. "What do you see?"

At the end of the pier sat a man in a drab blue jacket. Beyond him rose a sail boat with a dark red half-sail, heading out to sea.

A moment of silence. All movement and time stopped.

Edna raised her arm, pointing.

Corinne's hand covered her mouth, stifling an exclamation.

Mattie was frozen, her arms still stretched to the sides.

Then the moment was gone. The sailboat turned into the wind, the color disappeared, the man stood up from his seated position and disappeared into the sudden bevy of activity and people crowding the pier.

Mattie spoke softly. "For a moment, I thought it was him."

No one asked, "Who?" Mattie would not have been able to answer.

They found the store Charlie had told them about, where a young man behind the counter greeted them with a friendly smile and decidedly eastern accent. "Good afternoon, folks," he said. "Can I help you find something?"

"We need to buy hats and sunglasses." said Corinne. "It's easier than trying to travel with them."

"Right over this way," he said, leading them to a display at the front of the store. "Here for the day, or are you staying for a while?" he asked.

"We'll be here for a week," Mattie replied, "so we'll be needing some groceries as well."

"Dinner first," voted Corinne, now complaining of a very empty stomach.

"If you're ready for a treat, stop at The Water's Edge, right next to the pier. Ruthie has the best chowder on the Cape," advised the owner.

They were soon at the small diner he had described and seated on the open deck where they had an unobscured view of the water, and could listen to the soft swelling of the waves.

The chowder, thick with fresh clams and potato, was indeed the best Mattie could remember having. Corinne chose a creamy shrimp bisque with leeks, and Edna exclaimed over the grilled haddock.

"Let's take a container of chowder home with us for lunch tomorrow," suggested Corinne, looking covetously at Mattie's bowl. They lingered over the meal, breathing in the sea air. The constant movement of the water fascinated them. "It never stops," said Edna. "There is no movement in the desert, unless a lizard runs by."

"I'd better check on Julie and Edward. I wonder if they are out of Newark yet? Oh, my! I don't have my cell phone. I wonder if they've tried to call. I've been having so much fun I haven't thought about it."

Stopping at the grocer's on the way back, they purchased sweet rolls, cheese, and bananas for breakfast, crackers and specialty bread to go with the chowder, and two bottles of wine, enough to fill a bag for each of them to carry back to the bungalow.

They were half a block away from the cottage when they heard a familiar voice shouting in the quiet air.

"Mattie! Mattie! Thank God you are safe! Where have you been? Why don't you answer your phone? I've been frantic about you. We called the rental agency to get the key code, but they said it had already been picked up. Where were you?"

Edna took control, throwing her hands into the air and letting herself fall against a nearby light pole.

"Oh Julie! We couldn't find the shuttle to bring us from the airport, so we had to use our thumbs and hitchhike! We fought off three potential rapists who picked us up, then dumped us out on a deserted beach. We've been walking for the last two hours, looking for someone to help us find our address. We've lost our luggage and barely escaped with our lives! Oh, thank God you've found us!"

Julie's expression went from horror, to exasperation, as she listened, and finally to laughter. "You scared me to death, Mattie. Where have you been?"

"Come inside, Julie. We are all unpacked and nicely settled in." Mattie turned the key and swung the door open. "It's perfect, just perfect. We couldn't be happier."

"Oh Julie, I can imagine you were frightened and worried, but we are fine," Corinne chimed in. "Here, relax in this chair and I'll bring you a glass of wine. Oops! If this place has a cork screw. We forgot to check that!"

"And we have hot chowder ready for you to eat." Edna was anxious to make amends for her joke. "We were going to have it for lunch tomorrow, but you look like you could use something warm and soothing."

"Absolutely the best chowder you've ever tasted, I guarantee," promised Mattie.

"It smells wonderful," said Edward. "It's a good thing you ladies arrived when you did. I'd kept her from calling the police about as long as I could. Julie, you are the worst worrier in the world."

"So, young lady, where have you been? And didn't you think of calling Edna or Corinne when I didn't answer my phone?"

"There was trouble with an engine, so they landed us in Newark while they checked it out. It didn't take long, but we were two hours behind you when we arrived at the airport. We rented a car, since there was no shuttle, but had no idea where you were."

"Speak for yourself, Julie! I had a pretty good idea that our lovely ladies were finding their way around this delightful little town, and might have caught up with Robert Redford by now!"

After Julie and Edward had eaten chowder and unpacked their suitcases, they all made their way toward the water and soon found a place they could walk along the beach.

"What all do you have planned for the week?" asked Edward.

"Charlie gave us a quick tour of the town. He recommended that we sign up with the Bay Tour Company as soon as they have an opening. He said it's a great way to see the highlights and find our way around."

"Charlie?" asked Edward.

"Our shuttle driver! He was just great. Described everything along the way, told us where to get groceries, made sure the key was where it should be," explained Corinne.

"We want to do a whale watching trip sometime. That was just about number one on my list," Edna said.

"We'll call the Bay Tours first thing in the morning. Hopefully they will have room for us, then in the afternoon we can scout out some sailing outfits."

"Is it okay if we go around to some of these sailing companies with you tomorrow?" asked Julie. "Or is that too protective—too inhibiting to you?" She was half joking, but only half. She still felt a bit left out, as if she were stepping on their toes.

Mattie put her arm around Julie. "Of course. You're part of all this."

Corinne, always the one to think ahead, had brought a blanket over her arm. She spread it out on the sand, and they all sat down, watching the waves lap gently in front of them. Behind them, the sun had set and the light was beginning to fade. A few birds stalked close to shore, looking for a late snack, as the tide began to recede, leaving the wet sand covered with seaweed and scurrying crabs.

As the sky grew deeper gray and the air began to grow chilly, they gathered up the blanket. Corinne asked, "Is there anything special you want for breakfast, Julie? Edward?"

"No, I'm sure whatever you already picked up will be fine," said Julie.

"But I didn't see any coffee in those grocery bags. And what about a nice cup of hot cocoa before bedtime?" suggested Edward. "I guess I wouldn't mind walking for a bit and seeing the village."

So they started down the walk again. As they passed the bait shop, Julie, walking behind a couple of steps, stopped and gazed down the pier. Edward stopped and went back to her.

"See something?" he asked.

Pensively, Julie turned away from the pier. "For a moment, something looked familiar," she said. "Just the light, I guess." She laughed.

She put her hand into Edward's, shook her head slightly, and they caught up with the others.

The shop where they got groceries was small with narrow aisles and crowded shelves. It made Mattie think of the small delis she and Jake had shopped in when they spent the summer on the Mediterranean coast of Spain. They selected a few more items: meats and cheeses, fresh vegetables, and more fruit. With five of them to carry bags of groceries, they included dry staples they would need for the next week. Small amounts of sugar and flour, etc.

Back at the cottage, they again settled on the patio and watched the moon rise over the bay. At last, tired from their long trip and busy day, they said goodnight.

Chapter 10

"That's the man you want to talk to, right there," said the waitress, who had just taken her order at the counter, pointing toward the door.

Mattie had gotten up early, and finding everyone else sound asleep in the cottage, decided to go outside and watch the sunrise. Walking slowly down the boardwalk path, she soon found herself at the café where they had eaten the night before. Might as well order a breakfast sandwich before returning, she thought.

"Hey, Robert! Come here a minute," the woman called.

Mattie turned to see a tall man walking toward them with a slightly swaying gait, wearing a billed cap and a gray-blue jacket. His face was lined, deeply tanned, and his grey eyes were friendly. He smiled at Mattie, then looked at the woman behind the counter.

"What can I do for you, Ruthie?"

The clerk indicated Mattie. "This lady is from Arizona. She's never been here before and she wants to go sailing. She was asking about a reputable outfit close by." She turned to Mattie. "My name is Ruthie. This is Robert Redding. Robert ran the nicest sailing charter around for years. He's retired now, but still knows about all there is to know about the business. Sit down and have a cup of coffee with this guy and you'll soon learn what you need to know."

"Thank you. My name's Mattie. It's nice to meet you both."

"My pleasure," he said.

They went to a table together and sat down, coffee in hand.

"Arizona? I've never been there, though my wife had a sister who lived in Phoenix for a while. She always wanted us to come out for a visit. We tried to make arrangements a couple of times, but never could quite get it worked out. So what brings you to Shelton?"

"I'm here with some friends on vacation. We really want to go sailing, so I started by asking Ruthie here if she could recommend an outfit."

"There are some good ones around. If fact, I think they're all good. If they aren't, they fold up pretty quickly. The industry tries to police itself, and there are some fairly stringent laws and regulations in place."

"My niece will be glad to hear that! She is worried sick that I'll wind up out on the high seas with some idiot trying to make a buck off a stupid old woman." Mattie laughed.

"Sometimes these young folks do think we are pretty stupid, don't they?" He grinned as their eyes connected.

"Here's your sandwich." Ruthie set a plate of crisp fried potato with a thick slab of fish between two slices of dark bread in front of her.

"Wow! That looks wonderful!"

"Ruthie makes the best grilled cod around," declared Robert.

They were silent for a bit while Mattie cut the sandwich in half, and took a bite.

"So — what kind of sailing do you have in mind? Have you sailed before?"

"No," Mattie answered. "I know nothing about it at all. Never even been in a row boat. Just got it in my head that it would be fun to experience."

"Well, sailing can mean anything from a fully rigged ship, like the ones they used to cross the Atlantic hundreds of years ago, to a two-person sloop, just right for a bright, sunny, day's circle around the bay. And everything in between."

"I guess I had something at the smaller end of the scale in mind. I thought sailing was sort of an individual thing." Mattie didn't want to tell him that her vision was based on romantic movie scenes.

"You might want to get a feel for the thing with one of the group sailing tours around the bay. Friendly, safe, not too exciting, but you feel the wind in your face, and see how the turn of the sail controls the ship."

"I've always wondered how the wind could make the boat go in more than one direction. I mean, the wind blows straight, doesn't it?"

"It's all in how you set the sails. A sailboat is not quite the same as a kite." He pointed out the window. "See that one out there now? She's about to come around and approach the dock."

She watched, and sure enough, the boat turned toward the dock and came in slowly. Then, as it neared the dock, the sail shifted, the boat turned, and it started diagonally out into the cove again.

Mattie was silent. So, the boat could turn and reverse direction. Toward the dock. Away from it. Mattie blinked her eyes.

"Wow," she breathed. "How smooth. It's like a dance movement."

"Tell you what," he said, turning toward her and meeting her eyes. "When you finish that sandwich, we'll go down the beach a couple blocks to the marina and talk to the folks who run the rental there."

As they walked toward the marina, he pointed out different boats and their purposes. Some were fishing rigs, speed boats, and pleasure schooners. A couple of small sailboats moved slowly across the water. Mattie was fascinated.

They approached a sign that read "Secrest Bay Tours and Boat Rentals."

"This is Todd Secrest's operation. He knows what he is doing. Grew up on this pier, fishing and sailing with his father. There are more folks who make their living with tourist services than from fishing these days, so he focuses on sailing now. Got rid of the fishing rig several years ago."

"We talked about doing some deep-sea fishing, too, if we have time. A week seemed like plenty of time, but it will go by fast."

Robert waved to a young man working with some ropes on the deck of a good-sized boat.

"Hi, Todd. Got a minute to visit with a potential customer?"

The young man wound the rope into a neat pile, wiped his hands and came over to them, holding out his hand to Robert.

"Sure, Robert. Good to see you."

"This is Mattie, Todd. She's vacationing from the West. She's wondering about some sailing. Mattie, meet Todd."

Todd gripped her hand firmly.

"This is the right place, ma'am. What do you have in mind?"

"Nice to meet you, Todd." She smiled, then raised her hands in a gesture of surrender. "I need someone else to tell me where to begin. This is completely new to me," she laughed.

"I've got a group going out just after noon today that still has several seats available. It seats 22, and we take a two-hour tour around the cove and out into the open water. Let you get the feeling, and look over what some of the others are doing out there. I always advise getting on a sizable boat before trying a smaller one. They can be a little scary if you aren't even used to the feel of water under you. Ever get sea sick, or air sick?"

"I've never been on the water," she answered, "but no trouble with other forms of motion. I have four others with me. Can I make a tentative reservation for us? If you have a card, I could call if the others don't like the idea."

Todd pulled a card from his pocket and walked with them into the small hut which seemed to serve as an office. "What's the name?" he asked.

"Mattie Hampton. It will just be three, or maybe four of us. My niece won't want to come."

He wrote on a list and handed her the business card.

"Got you down for four passengers this afternoon at 1:30. Let me know by twelve if you want to scratch, will you? Folks often stop by after lunch."

Mattie and Robert started back toward the café, and Mattie looked at her watch.

"Oh my! I've been gone nearly an hour and a half! Julie will be frantic. And furious! And — oh, dear — I've left my phone at the house again. Excuse me, Robert." She took his hand briefly to say thank you. "I need to hurry. It was so nice to meet you, and you've been so helpful."

She turned away from him then and stepped off the boardwalk. She felt the uneven ground under her foot and tried to catch herself, but a sudden sharp pain in her ankle stopped her movement. As she crumpled toward the ground, Robert's arm caught her around the waist, holding her up.

"Take it easy!" he said. He helped her stand while she grimaced and leaned on him. "Take it easy," he said again. There was a bench ten feet away, and he half-carried her to where she could sit down on it. "There now. How bad is the pain?"

"O-o-w-w!" she cried. "Now what have I done?"

Chapter 11

"Is everyone up? Where's Mattie?"

"Still sleeping, I guess," answered Edna. "Time to wake her up."

"I thought for sure she would be the first one out the door this morning," said Corinne. "I'll get her." She went down the hallway toward the bedrooms.

"I suppose one of us had better call that sailing company," said Julie. "I do want to meet them and see what they have to offer. I want to be sure you're with someone reliable."

Corinne appeared again in the doorway, looking puzzled. "She's not there. Is she out in the yard?"

Julie went to the patio door. "I don't see her. Is she in the shower?"

"No," replied Edna.

"Did she have breakfast?" asked Edward, puzzled.

"Don't see any sight of it. Where could she be?"

Edward went to the front door, stepped out and looked to the right and the left. "Thought maybe she was out watching the sunrise on the beach. Don't see her anywhere."

"Mattie! Mattie!" Julie raced up and down the hallway, looking in every room. "Mattie! Where are you?"

"Now Julie, don't panic, she's just stepped out for a walk," comforted Edward.

"How could she do this? Doesn't she know she has other people with her? Corinne! Edna! How long have you been up?"

"I was first up, and having breakfast at 7:30," said Corinne. "What time is it now?"

"Almost 8:30," answered Edna. "Don't worry, Julie. It's like Mattie to get up and go out for breakfast before anyone else is up. Why, when we were in Sante Fe —"

"Oh, Edna, that was fifteen years ago! It's not the same now. She could get lost, have a spell of some kind, trip and fall."

"Try calling her, Julie. I'm sure she isn't far away." Edward sounded a little annoyed himself, now.

Julie pulled a phone from her purse and quickly made the call. She gripped the phone and held it to her ear. In a moment she said, "It's ringing." A couple seconds later, a chirping sound came from the cabinet in the kitchen. They all turned to see a black phone laying on the counter, making a noise that sounded more than a little like the background sounds at The Blue Wildebeest.

Corinne stepped over and picked it up. "She left her phone again. She never does that at home."

It kept making the noise as Julie slumped into one of the chairs in the living room. "Why would she do this?" She leaned her head forward and covered her eyes with her hands. "I'll never live through a week of this. At home, if I couldn't find her, I just called one of you," she said, looking at Corinne and Edna.

Edward took Julie's hand. "Well, you and I can take a little walk down toward the pier. She's probably having a bite of breakfast somewhere. That will give you something to do besides work on a nervous breakdown. Edna, Corinne, you wait here, and call us when she shows up. Come on, Julie."

He took her hand, led her to the door and opened it, to find Mattie slumped against a tall man who was reaching for the doorbell.

They stared at each other for a moment — those inside the house and the two standing on the porch.

"I suppose I'm in trouble again, Julie. I'm sorry about the phone. This is Robert Redf—I mean Redding. I twisted my ankle, but I think it will be alright. Oh, dear, you are angry, aren't you?"

Julie took a step forward and spoke through gritted teeth. *"Where have you been?"*

"I just went to have some breakfast. Then Ruthie introduced me to Robert, and he took me to meet Todd, who is going to take us all sailing this afternoon, and then . . ."

Julie erupted. "We aren't going sailing this afternoon and maybe never. Not with anyone, let alone some — some . . ." She shook as she glared at Robert, then turned back to Mattie. "We are going to find you a doctor and if you set foot out of my sight again I'm going to — to — "

"Oh, Julie, calm down," Edward interrupted. "Here, Mattie, have a seat." Edward took Mattie's other arm, and between them, he and Robert helped her to the couch. After they got her seated, Edward held his hand out to the stranger. "I'm Edward, and this is my wife, Julie, Mattie's niece. Thanks for helping her get back from — wherever she was. We seem to have a hard time keeping track of her."

"I'm glad I could help," replied Robert.

Edna stepped forward. "How bad is the ankle?"

"It hurts some," said Mattie, "but I'm sure it will be fine before long. It just doesn't want to have much weight put on it right now. Have we got any ice for an ice bag?"

"I'll get it," said Corinne and headed for the kitchen.

Julie knelt down beside Mattie, positioning herself between Mattie and Robert, then gently cradled the ankle. "We definitely need a doctor. These injuries just don't heal easily at your age, Mattie."

"There is a clinic about a mile down the road," offered Robert. "They have an excellent doctor, a Dr. White."

Julie tossed an icy glance up at him. "We aren't taking her to some out-of-the way clinic! Edward, will you call 911?"

"Oh, just let me have an ice bag for a few minutes! It will be fine." Mattie slapped Julie's hand away from her ankle.

Corinne returned with a plastic bag of ice wrapped in a towel. "Here, Mattie." She handed the bag to Mattie, then turned her attention to Robert. "Hello. I'm Corinne. Thank you so much for helping Mattie. We were getting real worried about her. I guess you live around here? Or are you a visitor like us."

"I've lived here all my life. Within 20 miles, anyway." There was silence for a moment, then he continued, uncomfortably. "Mattie was having breakfast at The Water's Edge when I happened in."

"I had just asked the owner, Ruthie, about sailing outfits, so she introduced Robert to me. He used to have a sailing business of his own," said Mattie. "He knows a good outfit right close, so we walked there to get some information. When we started back, I realized how long I'd been gone and started to hurry," continued Mattie.

"That's when she stepped off the walkway and twisted her ankle," finished Robert.

"She had no business going anywhere without us," snapped Julie, then turned back to Mattie. "Mattie, how could you be so irresponsible?"

Robert backed away toward the door. "I guess I'd better be going. You're safe now, Mattie."

"Wait!" cried Edna, as he opened the door. "Excuse us. We're just so surprised and have been worried. We just arrived yesterday afternoon, and aren't exactly feeling at home yet. Please — where is the clinic you mentioned?"

Robert glanced around at the others. "It's just about a half-mile up the shore, then another half-mile inland on North Cove Road. Dr. White is excellent, and he would refer you if you need more extensive help."

"Thank you, Robert, you've been so helpful," said Mattie. "I do hope we'll see you again."

Robert tipped his hat. "I hope so too, Mattie. Enjoy your sail. Take care of that ankle now."

Julie stood up and stepped toward him. "I'm sure we can take care of it. I'm sorry you've been troubled with all this." Julie ushered him through the door, and closed it behind him. His "Nice to meet you all," went nearly unheard.

Julie turned around and faced Mattie. "Oh, Mattie, how could you wander off by yourself? And running around with a complete stranger. What do you know about him? How foolish of you!"

"Julie — how could you be so rude? Didn't anyone ever teach you manners? I'm so embarrassed. I think I can handle this without your help!" She turned away from Julie. "Corinne, could you call a taxi, please? It would probably be best to have this looked at, though it really feels better already with the ice. Edna, please bring me my phone. I promise not to leave it out of my purse again. And Edward, please take Julie somewhere where I won't have to see her for a few hours until I calm down and figure out how to find Robert and apologize to him. I am absolutely humiliated."

"Mattie! Find him? Apologize? Be reasonable!"

"You be reasonable for a moment. I never treated you with less respect for your intelligence when you were a child. Yes, I should have left a note and taken my phone, and maybe you have a right to be angry with me. But that doesn't give you permission to be rude to a very kind gentleman who was only trying to be nice and helpful to a tourist in his hometown. I can't believe you treated him like that."

"I can't believe you would pick up with a complete stranger. You know nothing about him — you don't even know if this is his hometown, or if he is just floating across the country looking for lonely women to prey on. I can't believe I let you come here and —"

"Let me!" Mattie was shouting. "Let me! You don't have anything to do with 'letting me' do anything. I am not your child, and I am not senile. I will not have you thinking that I need your permission to do anything. I want you to go back to Philadelphia today and stay out of this holiday. Edward, get her out of here before I explode."

"Mattie! Julie! Stop this! Both of you need to just calm down!" Edward positioned himself between them. "Now count to ten, both of you, before you say another word." The room was silent for a moment, except for the heavy breathing of the two infuriated women.

"Charlie says he is just a couple of blocks away and will be here in a minute."

Julie stared at Corinne, "Charlie?" then turned to Mattie again. "Charlie? Who the hell is Charlie?"

Edna stepped forward. "Julie, let me explain. Charlie drove the shuttle from the airport. He took us on a nice tour of the city before he dropped us off here. He operates a local taxi service as well. He insisted we call him Charlie, and said to call him if we needed any information. He was really very nice."

"You haven't even been here 24 hours and already you're on first name basis with Charlie, and Robert, you've disappeared twice, and broken your ankle. How is it that I am not supposed to worry about you?" Julie wasn't shouting. She was screaming.

"Here's the taxi," said Edna, and opened the door.

Charlie, standing on the porch, tipped his hat and smiled broadly. "Good morning, ladies. I didn't expect an emergency call so soon! Twisted ankle, huh?"

"Julie," said Edward, "go get your purse while I help Mattie into the taxi. You and I will go for a walk."

"Oh, no, I'm going with Mattie and hear what the doctor says."

"I'll decide who's going to talk with the doctor," said Mattie, "and I prefer that you go with Edward — as far away as he is willing to take you."

"Let it go, Julie. She's right, and you don't need to fight about it at the doctor's office. Corinne and Edna will go with Mattie and between the three of them, they can get all the information we need."

"But, Edward —" Julie tried to protest.

"Then maybe you and Mattie will be able to listen to each other and talk civilly," he said over her objection. "Right now, you each need to calm down."

Julie turned away from them and went to the window, clenching her fists at her sides. Edward helped Mattie stand up, and with him supporting one side and Edna on the other, they started out the door.

"Really, I can manage, I think," protested Mattie, but she allowed them to support her. Corinne looked at Julie, and started to go to her, hesitated, then followed the others to the car. With Mattie settled in the back seat, Edward returned to the house, where Julie now stood fuming at the door.

Chapter 12

"Edward, how can you take her side?"

"Julie, I've never seen Mattie so angry before, and she had a right to be. You were more than just a little rude to that gentleman who brought her home."

"Gentleman? Edward, you don't know anything about him."

"I know that he brought Mattie here with an injured ankle, that he helped her out when she needed help. I know that she was introduced to him by a local café owner. I know that Mattie seemed to like him. I know that he was polite, and excused himself when he felt unwelcome. And I know he did not react to your rudeness by being rude in return. Now — what do you know about him, and what reason do you have to suspect him of being undesirable company for Mattie?"

"I just have a bad feeling about him. About this whole trip. Escapade. Mattie is so gullible, and expects so much more than could possible come true. She's already disappeared twice, proving that she isn't making good decisions. She is seventy years old, for heaven's sake. She has no business flying around the country with no one to take care of her except two other old ladies who are probably crazier than she is."

"Then why did you suggest the bucket list to her?"

"I was thinking of nice, little-old-lady things she and I could do together. Oh, I don't know what — maybe seeing a play on Broadway, or — or — I don't know — some secret wish, but not this. It's too dangerous."

"This fellow Robert didn't seem dangerous to me. In fact, he seemed more like a guardian angel this morning. Come on, Julie, let's go for that walk, and hope Mattie's ankle will be okay. Sounded like she had us booked on a sailing tour this afternoon. With Todd. You forgot to add him to her list of new acquaintances."

Julie saw no humor in the situation. "She is seventy years old, for heaven's sake."

"Yes, and you are treating her as if she were seven. She gave you more independence at seventeen than you are giving her credit for today."

Mattie fumed in the back seat of the taxi. "How dare she try to tell me what I can do or not do? Why did we even include them in this trip? And poor Robert — he was only trying to be nice and helpful. I can't believe Julie would act like that."

"Mattie, you frightened her to death. For the second time in less than twenty-four hours. You do have your phone with you — just in case you get lost again?"

"I wasn't lost, Edna. You know that. We don't have to hold each other's hands for the whole week, do we?"

Now Corinne chimed in. "A note, and carrying your cell phone isn't asking too much, even for old friends, but Julie isn't an old friend. She's a frightened little girl who doesn't want anything to happen to the one person she loves more than anything in the world. You know she's always been protective of you, and worried about you getting hurt."

"But to try and tell me what I am allowed to do? I won't have it! First thing you know she'll have me safely entrusted to a nursing home. Remember what happened to my neighbor, Mary, when her children decided she needed to be protected? I'll nip this in the bud, I tell you."

Corinne and Edna looked at each other with raised eyebrows.

"Julie would never treat you like —" began Edna.

"You bet she won't! She won't be given the chance!"

"Here's the clinic, ladies," said Charlie, pulling into the parking lot next to a small but modern looking building. "I'll help you in. Then, unless there is another call, I'll be right here when you are ready to go back. Calls are pretty slow this time of the day, but just call if I'm not right here. I won't be far away."

Forty-five minutes later, Charlie was helping Mattie into the car again.

"Just as I expected," she was telling him. "Just a mild sprain. Ice four times a day and a little rest and it should be fine by mid-week."

"That's lucky, little lady," he replied. "You don't want to spend your vacation on crutches. But you might be needing a taxi a little more than you would have otherwise. Tell you what — I'll make you a cut rate for the week, just so you won't have to put too much wear and tear on the boardwalk. I get the feeling that you want to cover a lot of territory the next few days."

"Thanks, Charlie, we appreciate that and will probably take you up on it."

Mattie's anger had calmed down, but she was still feeling defensive when they arrived back at the cottage. Edward and Julie were nowhere to be seen. Mattie called the Secrest's sailing service and canceled their seats for the afternoon. "We'll try to make it tomorrow," she said, explaining her injury.

Finally, she settled into a big comfortable chair, and felt tears well up in her eyes. "Everything seemed to be going so well," she sniffled. "I can deal with the injury, but not with Julie's stupidity."

"Now just be comfortable, and I'll get you a sandwich," said Corinne.

"You won't believe what a wonderful breakfast I had at The Water's Edge. Out-of-this-world grilled cod on a magnificent slice of the best bread I've ever eaten. Oh, I was so pleased and happy. Why did Julie have to ruin things?'

"Mattie, you had something to do with it, you know," scolded Edna. "We were all worried about you. Slipping out while we were all asleep wasn't so bad, but it had been almost two hours. Really, now, without your phone, what would you have done if you hadn't had Robert with you to help?"

"If I hadn't been with someone, I wouldn't have gone so far, and wouldn't have been so late," Mattie said in defense.

"And wouldn't have twisted your ankle. Julie's point exactly. You shouldn't have gone off like that without telling us." Edna was stern.

"Oh! Are you all going to be on her side?"

Corinne handed her the sandwich on a plate. "No, Julie was way out of line, too. But you both need to give a little, or it will ruin the entire vacation for all of us."

"She and Edward can just go home and leave us here to ourselves."

The door opened just then, and Julie and Edward walked in. Julie and Mattie looked at each other with drawn faces, so unlike anything they had ever faced each other with. Suddenly, Julie dissolved into tears and sank down beside Mattie on the big chair. They put their arms around each other and for a few minutes, just cried and held each other.

Chapter 13

The others moved silently into the kitchen area and left them alone.

"Whew! I hope they both come to their senses," said Edward.

"I've never seen Mattie so angry with anyone," added Corinne.

"What did the doctor say?"

"Just a slight sprain. He wrapped it, told her to put ice on it four times a day, and use a cane when she needs it for a few days. Not too much walking," said Corinne.

"I suppose we'd better keep them busy. We have the rental car for the week. We can take a drive around the cove, and have dinner somewhere. Unless it would be better to take that commercial tour you mentioned. Do you have that number? Do they have an afternoon tour?"

"Yes, that might be a better idea," said Edna. "That way, there won't be any disagreement over where to go. We can take the car later when we go out to dinner."

"I'll call and see if we can get on the tour, and what time it would be. I know they have one in the afternoon," offered Corinne.

"Let's make some sandwiches for the rest of us. Mattie has hers already."

The Blue Wildebeest

Edna and Edward laid the table with sandwich makings, and chips while Corinne made the call, then Edward approached the two in the living room.

"Lunch is served, ladies. I hope you're hungry. We have quite a layout."

Julie smiled at him, and at Mattie, then helped her aunt stand up with the cane. "Can you make it all right Mattie?"

"Yes, just let me have your arm. Corinne already brought me a sandwich, but I may want another."

As they made sandwiches and ate, the tension in the air subsided. Corinne announced that she had made reservations for the afternoon bus tour. She had called the taxi as well for a ride from the cottage to the departure area, she said, without mentioning Charlie by name.

When the taxi pulled up in front of the house, Julie asked, "You have your phone, Mattie?" Mattie's gaze turned icy and she lifted the phone from her purse. "I won't let it out of my purse again," she promised, softening. Julie smiled and together they all went out to the car.

They arrived with plenty of time to purchase tickets and get settled on the bus. Edward figured out how to use the head phones to listen to the tour guide, even though the driver assured them they would not need them.

"We'll be going through several townships this afternoon," the guide said. "Each of them started out as a small fishing village, or whaling port. Some gradually became sprawling townships, and finally they morphed into the mixture of small towns, wealthy gated communities and tourist areas that you see today." They enjoyed the commentary and history of each of the areas they passed through.

"We'll stop here at Truro and take a tour of the lighthouse," announced the guide. "It's the oldest and tallest of the lighthouses on Cape Cod. Those of you who want can make the climb to the top."

"Oh, good! I was hoping we'd get to do that," said Corinne.

"I read that there are several lighthouses on the Cape," said Julie to her companions. "These are dangerous waters, and they were needed."

Edward smiled at her and shook his head. "But we won't need one today, Julie. Just relax and enjoy the view."

The guide explained how the powerful Atlantic waves constantly eroded the shore line, until the lighthouse was in danger of tumbling into the sea. "In 1996, it was moved 450 feet west to where it stands now," he said, pointing ahead.

A short walk took them to a viewpoint where they could see the former location. They were stopped by a sign warning them to go no further: "Unstable Cliffs Ahead." Beyond they saw crumbling, sharp, sandy cliffs, and an unbroken view of the ocean.

"There's no land out there until you reach Portugal," said the guide, waving far out across the water. "Almost 3,000 miles."

Returning down the path to the lighthouse, they went inside, and faced the narrow circular stairway. Corinne hesitated.

"Maybe we don't need to go clear up," she said to Edna. "It looks like a pretty strenuous climb."

"Oh, pooh!" Edna laughed, starting up the steps.

Mattie, with her wrapped ankle, relaxed on a bench outside, while the others climbed to the top and took pictures to share with her.

"Maybe we can come back if your ankle is better before the end of the week, so you can go up too," said Julie, giving Mattie a hug. "The view is spectacular."

As the sun began to sink toward the west, they were delivered back to their starting point, hungry and tired. "If you are ready for dinner, that's one of the best oyster bars on the Cape," pointed out the guide, indicating an imposing yet charming building to the left. "Or if you want a steak, there is a great steakhouse just a block up. Of course, they have good seafood as well."

"What will you eat?" Julie asked all of them at once.

"Seafood, of course," echoed the three women.

"Seafood all week, for we won't get it again for months," added Mattie.

They chose the oyster bar, and later, even more tired but no longer hungry in the least, Charlie again delivered them to their door.

"It's nice to have Charlie so willing to help us," said Mattie, "but it would be so much more pleasant to walk wherever we can. In the morning, let's walk down to the café where I had breakfast this morning. It was very close, and so very good."

"We'll see," said Julie. "You need to take it easy on that ankle if you want it to heal."

"We have the rental car," said Edward. "We're paying for it so we may as well use it."

Chapter 14

Mattie rousted everyone out of bed in the morning at 7:00 a.m. "I'm hungry, and if you don't want me to hobble down the street by myself, you'll have to get up and join me."

Reluctant by different degrees, by 7:45 they had all joined her and were seated in the rental car for the short trip.

"Good morning, Ruthie." Mattie greeted the woman behind the counter as they entered the café. "I brought the gang with me today. I hope you have more of that grilled cod, and whatever kind of bread you served me yesterday."

"Welcome!" Ruthie smiled at the group. "We always have great bread, and whatever kind of fish you want. My bread-maker comes in real early and has the bread done and ready to serve by 6:00 a.m. when the guys start coming in. But — Whoa! You weren't hobbling with that cane yesterday. What happened?"

"Tried to get in a hurry. I should know better. I stepped off the walk and twisted the ankle. Luckily, Robert was still with me, and he helped me get back to the rental place." She glanced at Julie from the corner of her eye.

"You were in good hands," said Ruthie. "How bad is the ankle?"

"Just a light sprain, should be okay in a couple of days, but I'm going to miss walking up and down the sea shore for the time being. Do we need to order here, or can we have menus at the table?"

Ruthie picked up a handful of menus and led them to a table next to the window looking out over the water. "Shall I bring a pot of coffee to start with?"

They ordered breakfast, then turned their attention to the view out the window. The fishing dock stretched out into the cove, and several fishermen could be seen along its length. On the other side were a couple of boat docks with different size vessels waiting beside them. A few sailboats moved across the quiet water of the cove.

"I want to watch the sunrise from here one morning soon, if any of you lazy people will get up early with me. I don't want to run away again but if it's the only way I can watch the sunrise, well, so be it." Mattie seemed her old self again. Julie less so.

"It's not a joking matter, Mattie. You could have been lying on the street, unconscious, unidentified, and no way for us to be notified. It's not funny."

"Somehow, I think you would have found me. Anyway, as Ruthie said, I was in good hands."

"If you had been unconscious, that man wouldn't have known how to find us — even if he wanted to."

"What else would he have wanted? Julie, your imagination is running wild again."

"Why don't we ask him?" Edna stood up suddenly and waved to Robert, who had just entered the door. "Hello there, Mr. — Redding, is it? I'm afraid we didn't thank you properly for helping our friend yesterday. Will you join us for breakfast?"

Robert approached slowly, stopping several feet from the table. He tipped his hat and said, "Good morning."

"Please sit down," said Edna. She pulled a chair up between Edward and herself, across the table from Mattie. "I'm Edna, and this is Corinne. You know Mattie, and you met Edward and Julie at the house yesterday. It was so fortunate that you were there to help Mattie. We were all so flustered that I think we didn't react properly."

Robert still hesitated. "Thank you. I was just going to refill my coffee cup and take it out on the dock with me. The fish seem to be biting late this morning."

Edward stood up and made a little more room for the extra chair. "Please," he said. "I think we owe you an apology for being abrupt yesterday. We were so flustered, and Julie had been terribly worried about Mattie, hadn't you, Julie?"

"Yes, very worried — I — I couldn't imagine . . ." Julie was stammering. "She had just disappeared . . . Before anyone else was awake. In strange surroundings . . . She doesn't know anyone."

"I can understand," said Robert. "I'm sure I'd have been worried too." He turned to Mattie. "I'm glad to see you up and around this morning, Mattie. How's the ankle?"

"Much better this morning. Dr. White said to keep it wrapped for a day or two and use ice on it and it should be fine by the middle of the week. Thanks again for helping me home yesterday. Please do sit down." She smiled and gestured toward the chair. "Tell us about the fishing. What do you catch?"

"Have any of you ever fished from a pier?"

"Once, in Florida," said Corinne. "Art — my husband — got up every morning for a week. He only caught two small ones all week, but he had a great time."

Ruthie brought Robert a cup of coffee, and he sat down, rather on the edge of his chair. Conversation was cordial, but not the same easy friendliness that had marked Mattie's conversation with him the day before.

"So Arthur was a fisherman?" Edward asked Corinne.

"Strictly amateur. It was just something he remembered from his childhood, so when we were some place where it was the in thing to do, he would try it again. He never had his own equipment, so he always had to rent. Once we went out deep sea fishing and that was one of the most exciting things we ever did. He caught a huge tuna. We had it packaged and shipped home. We ate fish for a year, and shared with all our friends."

"I remember hearing about that," said Mattie. "We were living in Kansas City and didn't get any of your catch. Maybe we could try fishing for a big one while we're here. Though I don't know what we'd do with it if we caught anything."

"They will take it off your hands if you don't want it for yourself," said Corinne. "That would be fun, but we might have trouble finding an outfit that would take us out. They expect their customers to be men, or at least sure-footed females. I was younger then."

"Ooh!" chimed in Julie. "Is it dangerous?"

"Not if you're going out with a good crew," said Robert.

"Of course, anything could be dangerous if you act like a teenager and don't know what you are doing, I guess. I sat and watched, but I worried about Art at the time."

Julie's eyes got bigger and bigger as she glanced back and forth at the others as they talked. Finally, she burst out. "Oh, you wouldn't try something like that, would you?"

"Well, did we come all this way to sit on the beach and eat seafood? That's what we do at home, sit and watch sunsets and eat at the Blue Wildebeest. I'm for trying everything there is to try if it sounds like fun," said Edna. Then she added, "Of course, if it's safe."

"I'd be interested, if we could do it while we're here," said Edward.

"Oh, Edward!" is all Julie could choke out.

Edward ignored her and turned to Robert. "I'd like to see that pier fishing, too. Always wondered about throwing a fishing line into the ocean. What are the chances, in all that water, that a hungry fish would come by and bite my particular bait?"

"Believe it or not, all that water is full of fish," Robert said. "I fish off the pier next door there by the bait shop. Most mornings, I'm there by 5:30, and done by 7:00. This morning they started biting late, so I'm going back out for a while. Stop by sometime if you'd like to see how it's done. I'd be glad to see you any morning."

He asked Ruthie to fill the mug he was carrying and when she brought it to him, he stood up and excused himself. As he walked out the door, Mattie kept her eyes on her plate, hoping to hear something positive from her companions.

"Well," she said finally, "Let's start with something that was on our list to begin with. The sailing outfit that Robert introduced me to yesterday seemed very responsible and they have sailing tours every day. A nice big boat that holds twenty-five people. He said it was a good place to get a feel for what it is like to be on the water, and begin to learn how the sails work. Let's go talk to them after breakfast and see what you think. It's just a short way down the walk."

Julie was visibly relieved to be steered away from the even-more-dangerous deep-sea fishing idea. Conversation settled on the variety of breakfast dishes they had chosen, and they shared samples around the table. Corinne's adventurous selection of fresh fried oysters was the all-around favorite, even though Mattie didn't even want to try them.

"Too early in the morning to face an oyster," she said.

They thanked Ruthie for a wonderful meal, and went back to the car.

"Let's go down by the marina and talk to that sailing outfit," said Edward. "We could make a reservation for tomorrow then do some exploring the rest of the afternoon. What else does anyone have in mind?"

"We thought the town of Chatham sounded wonderful on the reviews we read at home," said Mattie. "They have a museum, a glass company, a light house. There were lots of things to see and do there that did not involve a boat."

"Yes," said Julie. "And the main street looked just charming."

At the marina they found Todd was out with a sail, but they visited with a woman who identified herself as Todd's wife. Satisfied with her manner and answers to all their questions, they made reservations for the next day.

Late in the afternoon, tired after taking in as much as they could of the Chatham area's attractions, they wandered along the shopping area, and ordered bowls of Portuguese kale soup in a tiny sit-down café.

"Unique! And very good," exclaimed Corinne.

"Who would have thought of Portuguese food on Cape Cod? But I guess they were among the earliest settlers on the Cape."

Tipping his bowl to get the last of the tasty broth, Edward said, "I think I will get up early tomorrow morning and go down to the fishing dock. Robert seemed genuine about the invitation to join him — as if he would welcome the company. I might decide to buy a fishing rod if I like it and think I'd have time to try it again."

"That would be too early for me to get up this time," said Edna. "Mattie didn't let us sleep in this morning."

Julie smiled. "I think the afternoon sail will be enough excitement tomorrow. And if we don't eat those cranberry bagels we bought, they won't be any good."

"I'll go with you," said Mattie. "I want to watch the sunrise."

Julie seemed to reconsider. "Well, maybe —"

"I'll have bagels with you and Edna, Julie," interrupted Corinne. "With a pot of coffee, I'll be happy for the morning."

Chapter 15

Mattie, once again the first one up in the morning, tested her ankle gingerly and found it surprisingly comfortable to move around if she used the cane.

It wasn't long before Edward appeared in the doorway.

"Don't fix anything here," he said. "I can't wait to try something else from Ruthie's kitchen."

When they arrived at the Water's Edge, they were able to quickly pick out Robert from among the half dozen fishermen on the pier. Juggling sandwich and coffee, they made their way to where he was seated on a small cooler.

"Good morning!" His smile assured them they were welcome. He offered Mattie his seat on the cooler, and she accepted graciously. Soon, Edward and Robert were engaged in a lively conversation about the gear he was using and the varieties of fish to be found in these waters. The eastern sky was brilliant with orange and magenta colors playing on the low clouds. Mattie pulled out her camera and took pictures of the men with the rosy sunrise behind them.

"Your sunrise measures up pretty well with what we see in Phoenix. It's beautiful."

"Some mornings are more impressive than others," Robert smiled back. The color slowly faded into bright sunlight, and Mattie found herself tiring. She excused herself to go back inside the café.

"Okay, but you'd better be there when I come in," joked Edward. "Julie would kill me if I lost you again."

She laughed and promised to stay where he could find her.

Inside the café, Ruthie was busy with several customers. Mattie selected a handful of tourist brochures from the rack at the door, and took a cup of coffee to a table by the window. She looked over the advertisements for deep-sea fishing, whale watching, evening dinner sails, tours of the bay, trips to Martha's Vineyard and Nantucket, jet skis, parasailing — so many things to do on the water. She wondered what Julie would enjoy. She would probably like to see Martha's Vineyard and Nantucket if they didn't involve a boat ride to get there. There was information on several museums, a cranberry bog, the Sandwich glass company, and potato chip factory. And shopping, of course. Julie always liked souvenir shopping when they had traveled before.

An hour later, the two men joined her in the café. "Robert thinks we could go deep sea fishing tomorrow afternoon from Provincetown." Edward smiled wryly as he sat down. "Do you think you could keep Julie busy long enough for me to go? Unless you would want to go along."

"Edna sounded like she'd like to go along, but I think Corinne and I could find something Julie would like. I was just looking through these brochures with her in mind."

"I wonder what you three would be doing now if Julie wasn't along? I hope you don't let her slow you down too much."

The three conversed easily, and Edward asked Robert to join them on the sailing tour in the afternoon.

"I'd be glad to join you," Robert responded, "if I'm not crashing the party."

"You're more than welcome," said Edward, and Mattie agreed enthusiastically.

"We'd love to have you join us. It's the two o'clock sail at Todd's."

"Julie, you don't have to come."

Mattie had taken a nap after the morning trip to the pier. She and Julie were alone in the kitchen, preparing snacks and drinks for the afternoon.

"I'd go crazy not knowing what was happening out there. It would be worse than drowning with you."

Mattie sighed and shook her head. "I should have realized you were developing a phobia that first time when you panicked at the second-grade picnic."

"Mattie, this isn't some unreasonable psychological phobia!" Julie said, slapping mayonnaise forcefully on half a hoagie bun. "It's a logical fear of something that can — and does — happen in real life." She stopped and turned toward Mattie. "Have you really forgotten?"

"Airplanes crash occasionally," Mattie countered, meeting her eyes. "Cars go off the road. Horses throw off their riders. But you still ride them. It is a phobia, Julie."

"It took my parents from me, Mattie." They stared at each other. "I don't think I could go on if I lost you too."

Mattie's eyes softened and she reached for Julie's hand, still holding the hoagie. "Someday you'll have to, Julie. You know that."

Julie dropped the bun on the table and turned away.

Mattie went to her side. "I understand, Julie. You were a six-year old child, and your parents went off to a strange place and never came back. You were so frightened, lost, and lonely. Maybe it was a healthy thing for you to put all your fears onto the idea of a boat, so you could face the big hole in your life." She paused. "But Julie, it's time to let go."

"I can't, Mattie." Julie kept her eyes turned away.

"Well, I can't make you let go of it. But you can't expect it to control my life too."

Chapter 16

"Hello, Todd," Mattie said as the group arrived at the dock. "These are my friends, Edna, and Corinne. And this is my niece, Julie, and her husband, Edward. I guess we are ready for our — my — maiden voyage."

"Glad to have you," said Todd. "Some of you have sailed before?"

"A few times," said Corinne. "Art and I even took a three-hour trip on a tall-mast sailing rig once. It was exciting, to say the least."

"All my water adventures have been powered with an engine, not the wind," said Edna. "So you do everything with the sail?"

"We'll talk about that a little this afternoon," said Todd, "but if you come back for a trip on a smaller rig, we'll demonstrate in more detail. We can spend a whole afternoon just sailing in the cove here, learning the basics. Today we'll leave the cove and go up the coast a little way. We'll pass a lighthouse, and might see some of the seals, though we aren't allowed to get too close."

"Robert is coming, too," said Mattie. "He is supposed to meet us here."

"Here he comes now," said Todd. "You'll learn even more with him along. Robert likes to explain stuff."

There were rows of two seats on the boat. Edna and Corinne were first on and took seats at the front. Mattie sat behind them, with Robert at her side, while Edward guided a trembling Julie into the seat behind them.

Mattie sat next to the rail. The boat motored slowly away from the dock, passing the two other boats moored beside them, making their way beyond the end of the pier. Edna and Corinne were intent on the forward motion of the boat. As they reached open water, Todd raised the sail and it whipped open. Mattie gasped at the sound, as the canvas filled with air. She stared at the points of the sails against the blue sky. Her heart began to pound with excitement, and she leaned out to the side as far as she could. She reached automatically for the hand nearest to her. It was Robert's.

He placed his other hand on top of hers, and chuckled. "You'll love this," he said. "Just relax and breathe deep."

For a few minutes, she didn't speak, didn't want to break the spell. Then she turned back toward Edward and Julie. Julie was staring at where Robert's hand still covered her own. Julie's face was hard. She looked as if she were chiseled out of stone.

Mattie turned completely around to face them, moving both of her hands to the back of her seat as she did so.

"Oh, Julie. Just look at all the different colors and sizes of boats, and the way they are going different speeds and directions. This is wonderful."

Julie smiled weakly, and placed her own hand on top of Mattie's. The boat rose and fell softly on the water, then gave a small lurch to the side as they crossed the wake of another vessel — just a quiver, Mattie thought — and Julie crumpled into Edwards's arms. He held her tightly. "It's okay, sweetheart. We're on the water. It's going to go up and down a little."

Julie sat up again and checked the buckle on her life vest.

"Oh, darling, I wish you could enjoy this as much as I am!" Mattie said.

"Me too," whispered Julie.

Todd began to talk to them about the activity on the boat: setting and trimming the sails, the main sail, and the jib. He guided the motion of the boat to the left and then back to the right, briefly describing parts of the vessel and his actions.

Robert elaborated with details of what Todd was doing. "The boat can't go directly into the wind, but by tacking, which is zig-zagging slightly from one side to the other — well, 45 degrees to the left of the wind and 45 degrees to the right of the wind, it will move the boat upwind. That's done by turning the boat and adjusting the sail. It produces a pretty straight-forward motion. It's a difficult but necessary maneuver."

He turned to include Edward and Julie in the conversation. Julie remained ramrod-still, her face taut. Edward had his arm around her. Julie looked as if she wished she were anywhere in the world except where she found herself right now. Mattie wished, for a moment that she could comfort her, but then she turned back where she could feel the wind in her face. Julie would have to face her own fears.

Mattie leaned forward toward Edna and Corinne in front of her. "Isn't it marvelous?"

Corinne answered, "Never thought I'd be on a sailboat again. But this time I'm learning more about it as well."

Edna's face was glowing. "This is wonderful, Mattie." She lowered her voice. "How is Julie doing?"

"Rough, but she'll survive."

Robert looked at them quizzically, but said nothing.

Edward asked questions about mechanical details — man questions, Mattie thought, though she found the extra detail fascinating as well.

"A lot of this becomes automatic," said Todd, as Robert finished explaining one technical maneuvering. "Everyone who sails has to know how to do it, but Robert knows how to explain it when it is new to you."

Todd showed them the lighthouse, pointed out mansions of the famous Cape residents, and identified the historical areas. By the time they returned to the dock, they knew a great deal more about the area than they had before.

As they re-entered the cove, and neared the dock, Mattie commented. "I love the way you can be moving so swiftly, yet it's so silent. The movement of the water at the side sounds like the waves on the shoreline of a lake."

They pulled up to the dock again, smoothly and quietly. Julie smiled wanly as they moved off the boat, clinging to Edward like a small child.

"Julie, you did it!" cried Corinne. "You were so brave."

Julie nodded her head. "Can we go home now? I need to lie down."

"I'll take you home," said Edward. "Robert can take the girls and try that restaurant Todd recommended. We'll have the rest of that chowder at the house."

Julie looked at Mattie, then at Robert. "Well — but — maybe . . ." she stammered, then Edward put his arm around her and turned her away from the dock. "Come on, sweetheart. Enough for you today."

Chapter 17

Mattie watched as Julie and Edward walked away, then turned to the others. "I can't wait to go again," she said. "When can we get on a smaller boat?" she asked Todd, who was looking through papers on a clipboard.

"It's kind of a busy week," he said. "But our six-person scoop is available on Thursday in the late afternoon," he said.

"Great," said Mattie. "We'll see you then."

Robert drove them back on the main road that had brought them into Shelton, then up the coast a few miles, to a restaurant perched near the top of a hill overlooking a rugged coastline.

"I hope we can have an outdoor table," said Corinne. They were soon seated where they could watch and listen to powerful waves crashing against the rocky cliffs below. Todd had warned them it was expensive, but worth every penny. The view was fantastic, strolling musicians provided extra ambiance, and the food was superb. They lingered on the terrace with drinks after dinner.

"First time I've been here in ten years," said Robert. "Since before my wife died."

"The Blue Wildebeest will have to work hard to impress us after this," said Corinne.

"The Blue Wildebeest?"

"It's a restaurant in Phoenix not far from where I live. It's our favorite place to have lunch, coffee, or just spend a couple hours relaxing with a glass of wine or a snack and sharing thoughts," answered Mattie.

"The décor is totally incongruous with the desert outside. There is a section that looks, sounds and feels like a rain forest, and we feel like we're back in some distant time and place," added Edna.

"The Serengeti Room is quieter and it really does make me feel like I'm on safari again," Corinne said.

"And another area that gives me the creeps because it's so jungle-like," said Mattie. "I expect a jaguar or a python to drop from the trees any minute. But it's still fun."

Robert laughed. "I was in the Florida Everglades once, but can't say I really liked it much. Creepy, like you said. Guess that's the most exotic place I've experienced. The time I spent in the service was the only time in my life I've been far from the ocean."

"And I've never lived near it, though most of my favorite places to visit or vacation were on the coast. Jake and I loved Carmel in the 60's. I probably couldn't even afford to visit there now."

"I always thought the best place to vacation was in my own back yard, or on the boat. Mary and I took some long sailing trips after the children were grown." Robert smiled wistfully. "We'd take the boat south where it stays warm at the end of the busy season, then tie up where we could find a dock available at night, and sail during the day. Two, three weeks — maybe a month before we headed home."

"Wow! I can't imagine being on the water for a month. You wouldn't necessarily have smooth sailing weather for that long, would you?"

"Right. We ran into rough weather occasionally, but we avoided the hurricane season. I've always wondered about how people can live in the desert. It's hot and dry there all the time, isn't it? Water is such a big part of our way of life. I just can't imagine a dry landscape."

"Julie feels the same way about the desert. But it has its own fascination."

"The buttes have been sculpted by the wind and sand into fascinating shapes," said Corinne. "Then they're coated with black and reddish colors called desert varnish. Takes thousands of years. The sea is constantly moving, changing, but the desert is . . . well . . . eternal."

Edna nodded in agreement. "I've gone hiking on a few occasions — always with a small group and a guide. It's an overwhelming feeling out there, like you're surrounded by spirits. You know you could not survive on your own for more than a few hours. Makes you face your own mortality."

"Get far enough out at sea to not be able to see the land, and I suppose it's the same feeling," said Robert. "You are simply overwhelmed by the immensity of the water."

"Either one would put you in touch with your spiritual side, I'm sure," said Mattie.

"Why is Julie so afraid of the water?"

"It isn't the water itself she fears. She swims and enjoys it. It's the boat. She is terrified of boats," Edna clarified.

"She was six when her parents took a two-week trip to Malaysia," Mattie continued. "They left Julie with me. Their group was on a ferry that capsized. There were some survivors, but Tom and Meg's bodies were never found."

"That would be awfully hard for a six-year-old," said Robert.

"Julie clung to me for months, but I didn't realize she had also developed a phobia of boats until the end of the school year. Her class went on a picnic at the lake and the trip included a boat ride. Julie panicked. Not only did she refuse to get on the boat herself, she became hysterical as her classmates and teachers prepared to board. They had to call me to come and get her before the picnic could continue."

"Remember how she got so upset even with a picture of a boat?" said Corinne.

"I thought she would work through this with the counselor she was seeing at the time. She adjusted in time to school work and friendships, but the fear of boats, and her dependence on me, never seemed to go away."

"Just getting on the boat today was a huge milestone for her," said Edna.

"Yes, but she said it would be more frightening to have me go alone."

"She's very protective of you."

"So much of the available activities here involve boating, it's hard to know what to do with her," said Mattie.

"Julie would enjoy Martha's Vineyard and Nantucket if it weren't for the ferry ride over."

"You can get to them by air," said Robert, "but it's costly."

"Really? We thought the only way was by boat."

"No, Barnstable Airport in Hyannis serves both islands. You can even fly between them."

"Hmm . . ." said Mattie. "We can call in the morning and see if there is room on a flight any time this week."

Chapter 18

The next morning, Mattie found she could walk without the cane. She clattered pots and pans and dishes around in the kitchen, hoping to wake someone up. Dressed in her sleek new capris and a light jacket over a striped tank top, she was eager to see what the day would bring.

When Edward came into the room, she had the coffee made and breakfast choices set out. He filled a cup and peeled a banana.

"Robert said that it's possible to fly from the airport in Hyannis to the Islands," Mattie told him. "I'll bet Julie would enjoy seeing Martha's Vineyard or Nantucket if we could get her on a flight. We could take the ferry and meet her there."

"That's great news! I know she was wishing she could see the islands. I thought maybe after the first ride, she would feel better about traveling on the water, but she had trouble sleeping all night. Just the word 'ferry' throws her into a panic."

"Cape Cod just isn't the right vacation spot for someone with her phobia."

Edward reached for the phone book lying on the counter. "I wonder how the airport is listed."

"Robert said it was Barnstable Municipal Airport in Hyannis. They are probably all booked up for the week, but it's worth a try."

Edward thumbed through the pages, then touched numbers on his phone. After a few inquiries, he put his hand over the phone and looked up at Mattie. "They've had a cancellation for tomorrow morning to Martha's Vineyard. Should we take it, or wait to ask the others?"

"Grab it!" said Mattie. "Executive decision! If they want to take part in the planning, they will just have to get up earlier in the morning."

Edward finished the phone call, then said, "I'd best go explain the plan to Julie, so she can work her head around the idea before everyone is up. I think she will be all right with it, if she takes a minute to let it sink in. She's never comfortable with surprises. She'll want you to fly with her, but they only had one seat available."

By mid-morning, they were all ready for the day's activity. They would drive up to Provincetown, sight-seeing along the way. Robert would meet them for lunch in Provincetown, then he and Edward would go on a three-hour deep sea fishing excursion, in spite of Julie's apprehension of both the fishing trip and Edward's companion.

"How do you know he knows what he's doing?" Julie asked Edward.

"Oh, Julie, stop fussing about Robert. I'm enjoying his company and know-how. And it's a commercial fishing outfit, for heaven's sake."

They ate luscious lobster rolls at MacMillan Wharf, then Edward and Robert headed to the fishing boat. The women visited the museum on the pier. It featured items recovered from the pirate ship Whydah which sank off the coast in 1717, and recounted fascinating but conflicting stories of the ship, the sailor turned pirate, and his doomed love affair. Leaving the museum, they purchased a pamphlet for a walking tour and began to explore the busy tourist area. They browsed through art shops and looked for the blue plaques on many of the buildings, which explained the historical significance and hinted at intriguing legends and stories.

When they began to tire, they got on the trolley and enjoyed a narrated tour which included a stop at the Pilgrim Monument, a 250-foot round tower commemorating the Pilgrims' first landing.

"They stopped here before they went on to Plymouth Rock," said Edna. "It was their very first look at the new world. Of course, they didn't have this tower to look from. The guide said that on a clear day you can see Boston's skyline from the top."

"Let's climb up," said Julie excitedly.

"Yes!" agreed Edna.

But Corinne held up her hand. "It's too much. I don't think we could make it."

"You are the one who wanted lighthouses. The view from up there would make the lighthouse look puny. Let's do it!"

Corinne locked eyes with Edna and spoke firmly. "No, Edna. It's too much."

Julie looked from one to the other. "Well, maybe — but we could always turn around half way."

Edna and Corinne glared at each other, until Mattie intervened. "The trolley isn't going to stop for that long anyway. Why are you arguing about it?"

When the trolley returned to the central area, they still had time for a short tour of the dunes along the Province Lands, part of Cape Cod National Seashore. Nestled among the desolate shifting sands and beach grasses were small, primitive shacks originally built as lifesaving posts. Driftwood and other found beach materials were incorporated into the ramshackle structures, many of which floated on pilings to keep them above the ever changing sands. These were the famous dune shacks later used by artists and writers as hermitages: Eugene O'Neill, Norman Mailer and Jackson Pollack among many others.

"Wow!" said Corinne. "With nothing else to do, even I could write a book if I lived here."

Edward and Robert were waiting for them at the wharf when they returned.

"We've provided dinner," said Edward, "as all sea-going fishermen should do."

"I hope you are going to cook it, too," laughed Julie.

"Actually, the crew took it to a restaurant just down the way. For a price, they'll fillet it, cook it, and serve it with a side dish and a bottle of wine."

They made their way down the street to the restaurant and shared their adventures of the day. The men, as well as the women, seemed to have enjoyed themselves immensely.

"I hope you will come with us to Martha's Vineyard tomorrow," Edward said to Robert. "Your knowledge of the area makes everything so much more interesting."

"Thanks! I'd love to join you. I haven't been to the Vineyard for a long time. You know, it's been really nice meeting you folks."

Robert raised his glass in a toast to his new friends, and the others followed suit. But Julie did not smile.

Chapter 19

Julie was dropped off at the airport in the morning, and the others continued to Hyannis, where they boarded the ferry for Martha's Vineyard. Julie was waiting for them at the dock when they disembarked in Oak Bluffs, having caught a cab from the plane.

"We always came over to the island for the day at least once during the summers while the kids were still at home," Robert said. "The Flying Horses Carousel — it's the oldest working carousel in the country — was a favorite when they were little. They still have the brass rings to catch to win a free ride."

They decided not to wait in the long line to ride the carousel, but they were able to get close enough to marvel at the horses' radiating glass eyes and flowing horsehair manes.

"I want to see the gingerbread cottages," said Julie. "The person sitting next to me on the plane said not to miss them."

"Coming up next," said Robert. "This area started out as a church camp with tents in the 1800's. Most of the cottages are privately owned now, and many are available to rent if you plan far enough ahead."

Walking through the gingerbread cottage neighborhood the women were not disappointed. Like a dollhouse village, pastel colors and bright candy hues defined the closely spaced, whimsical, gingerbread-trimmed cottages. Filigreed balconies, tiny gardens, inviting rocking chairs on nineteenth century porches, and ornate, wooden scroll work created a fairy tale atmosphere.

They rented a van and Robert drove them around the picturesque island. The dramatic cliffs at Aquinnah, with the lighthouse in the background, were breathtaking. "The cliffs are eroding several feet per year, so they've just finished moving the lighthouse about 120 feet or so from the original location to where it is now. It was ready to tumble off the edge," Robert said, explaining the construction still going on. "We could walk down to the beach, but it might put a little strain on Mattie's ankle. We can stop at a closer beach later."

They had drinks on the patio of one of the diners with a wide view of the ocean all around. The breeze brought the salty air and the sound of crashing waves to their table.

They stopped to relax awhile at the beach near Menemsha, then drove past miles of stone walls dividing fields and surrounding houses in the Chilmark area. They recognized scenes there from the film *Jaws*, and more as they drove through Edgartown.

"I still get shivers when I think of that movie," said Corinne, as they passed another location featured in the film.

Arriving back in Oak Bluffs, they headed to the waterfront. Choosing a small but picturesque diner built on a pier overlooking the water, they each ordered a lobster dinner. The women laughed at each other's clumsy attempts to get at the succulent, buttery flesh in the claws, before turning their attention to the rich, meaty tails.

As they lingered over drinks and watched the boats returning to docks, Mattie asked Robert, "Have you always lived in the area?"

"Born right down the coast about ten miles from where you folks are staying," he answered.

"I'll bet you learned sailing and fishing pretty young," said Edward.

"Fishing has been more of a retirement thing," he answered. "But I learned to sail as a kid, and then worked in the business through high school."

"Ruthie told me you used to run your own sailing company."

"When I married Mary, we decided we wanted to run our own business, so we opened up Rob & Mary Sailing tours. We had a couple of little boats to take the couples who wanted a small, personal trip. Experienced sailors could rent them by the hour and go out on their own."

"That might have been risky," said Edna.

"First they had to prove to us they knew what they were doing. Then we had the larger schooner that would carry twelve passengers besides ourselves." He paused, seemingly lost in thought. "It was a good business. Mary and I enjoyed it and practically raised our two children on the boat dock."

"Wow! That must have been hard," said Corinne.

"Sounds dangerous to me," said Julie.

"Have you been alone for long?" asked Corinne, ignoring Julie.

"Mary passed away ten years ago, when we were both sixty. We'd looked forward to retiring, having the grandchildren — and great grandchildren — spend the summers. Anyway, I kept up the business till I was sixty-five and eligible for Medicare — some of you know that story, I'm sure. Running the business by myself was too much, but retirement's been — well, not busy enough, sometimes."

"Seems like there is plenty to do if you like water and good food," laughed Edna.

"It's been a good life," he agreed. "I still have a sailboat — it's with my son right now, down close to Providence. His kids and grandkids are visiting him from Tennessee, and he likes to take them out. He doesn't have a rig of his own, so I let him have mine when they are with him. They usually spend a couple weeks every summer. I go down and spend some time with them, then leave the boat with them. He'll be bringing it back sometime soon." His eyes brightened and he looked at Mattie. "You know, I could take you all out on it, if he gets it back while you are still here." He took a deep breath. "Wow! I haven't talked that much for a year."

"I'll bet the girls will take you up on that offer," said Edward.

"Of course, we've already sailed once, and we're planning another outing with Todd," pointed out Julie.

"Well, talk about being in competent hands, sweetheart. You were so worried about them sailing with someone unreliable."

There was an edge to their voices. Edna changed the topic.

"I'd like to go to the beach and swim tomorrow," she said. "How would you all feel about that in the morning?"

"Great!" said Julie.

Corinne looked at Edna "Are you sure you are up to swimming in the ocean? You haven't done that for a long time. I don't think I could battle the waves."

Strange question, thought Mattie. Edna is a strong swimmer.

"Oh, I won't try to reach one of the islands." Edna laughed. "I know I'm not as strong as I used to be. Just a nice easy swim with the tourists."

"I know a beach on the bay side that is usually calm, and not too crowded," said Robert.

"Can you come along and bring your car?" asked Edward. "I don't think we could all squeeze into the rental. But if we took both cars we'd be comfortable even with towels and coolers."

They saw Julie off to the airport, then checked in at the ferry again. They jostled the crowd until they found three seats together. "Ladies first," said Edward.

"There is plenty of room outside on the deck," said Mattie. "I'll go out there. I want to feel the wind in my face again."

"Do you mind if I join you?" asked Robert.

"Please do," she answered. Edward sat down with Edna and Corinne, and Mattie and Robert made their way outside. The rows of benches on the deck were mostly empty. They moved to the front of the boat and sat down just as a half-moon rose over the horizon. A few low-lying narrow cloud bands gave it an ethereal look.

"It is beautiful, isn't it?" said Mattie, breathing in the rich, salty air.

"I never tire of just looking out over the water," he answered. "It is never quite still, yet it calms the nerves, eases whatever may be bothering you." He paused. "Your name. Mattie. Is it—"

"Short for Matilda," she finished his question, and laughed. "Good old fashioned name. Even sixty years ago, they never got my name mixed up with anyone else in school. I shortened it to Mattie when I was a teenager."

"I named my first boat Matilda," he said. "I was nineteen years old, and had just seen *On the Beach*."

"I remember that movie. It stayed with me for years. The song was so haunting."

"I hummed Waltzing Matilda that whole summer, working on a fishing boat. By the end of August, I'd saved enough to buy a small second-hand rig. I named her Matilda, put all my belongings in her and sailed down the coast."

"Did you get all the way to Australia?" she asked with a smile.

He laughed. "Not hardly! But I did learn my way around the Florida coast and outlying islands. Stayed there for two years. That's where I really learned to sail. When I came home the following summer, I was pretty proficient, and ready to settle down."

"And you've been here ever since?"

"Pretty much. I put in four years with the Navy, just before things got too hot in Vietnam. Guess I was lucky to be between Korea and 'Nam. I've had a lot of friends over the years who saw action one place or the other."

"The movie — *On the Beach* — made activists out of Edna and me. We demonstrated, joined marches. If Julie knew all the things we did those years — I don't know if she'd be less concerned about anything we might try today, or if she would really try to keep us down."

"Some things are best kept secret from the young ones, aren't they?" he quipped.

"I just wish Julie could relax, and enjoy this time like I am. We really almost came to blows the first couple days. Now it's just sort of a cold standoff. I'm not sure which is worse."

On the plane, Julie leaned back in her seat and closed her eyes. She thought about Mattie on the ferry, and felt her chest tighten and her heart speed up. It was such a brief flight but the morning trip had felt like hours, even with the friendly passenger beside her who kept talking about Martha's Vineyard, not letting her dwell on her fears. Now the seat beside her was empty and she was tired from the long day. She wanted to sleep, but her mind filled with visions of the ferry being tossed on violent waves, Mattie hanging on to the rail. She willed herself to stop thinking, and slowly the urge to sleep won over.

A man sat down in the seat beside her. She looked at him curiously. He smiled. His young face was friendly, familiar looking. "She's right, you know. It is a phobia," he said. How did he know about it, she wondered?

"Don't worry. She'll be fine," she heard him say, as she drifted back into sleep. "I promised her I'd send a sailboat."

Chapter 20

"It's some ways to walk," Robert said, as they got out of the cars. The morning air was heavy with the scent of the ocean wafting up from the blue water below them. The narrow grassy area next to the parking lot, where a few stunted wind-swept pines struggled to grow, gave way to a sharp drop-off. From there a wooden stairway led down to the beach.

"It's beautiful," said Corinne standing next to the car. "And not as crowded as I expected. The beach down close to the marina was absolutely packed when we walked down there."

The women picked up towels and blankets and the men carried the cooler and umbrellas. They walked down the steps and onto the beach, then picked a place where the sand was dry, and not too close to the families with frolicking children. They spread out blankets, listening to the sound of the gentle waves, punctuated by the sharp cries of the sea birds.

"There's not usually much of a current here," Robert said. "I guess you all swim?"

"Edna competed till she was fifty," said Mattie. "I swim in the pool, but don't get past my waist in the ocean."

"My competition days have been over for a long time. I'll just take an easy dip."

"Don't go out far, Edna." Corinne's voice had an unusual edge to it. "I'll be looking for shells at the edge. What about you, Julie?"

"Edward and I love the ocean. It's so playful. Robert, I think you found us a wonderful spot." Mattie smiled at Julie's friendly comment to Robert.

Mattie tiptoed into the water and squealed as it lapped up higher on her legs and then engulfed her waist. Edna moved quickly out further, and dived under the rolling waves.

"Oh, look, here's a beauty!" cried Corinne, holding up a shell that was only slightly battered. They swam and splashed according to their abilities, shouting to each other over the sound of the waves, and picking up bits of driftwood, shells and rocks. In two's and three's, they ran back and forth to the umbrella, got drinks from the cooler and ate snacks.

As the sun rose higher above them, they began to get hungry for lunch, and decided it was time to leave.

"Just one more quick dip," said Edna. "This has been wonderful, and I may never get another chance!" She laughed and ran back toward the water.

They packed the food and drinks back into the cooler. They folded the towels, trying futilely to shake the sand from the blankets, laughing and talking.

Edward was wrestling with the umbrella when he suddenly stopped, staring toward the water.

"Uh-oh," he said, dropping the umbrella. "Edna's in trouble."

He began to run across the sand. Mattie turned to see Edna knee deep in the water, struggling to stay on her feet. A wave hit her from behind and she stumbled, seeming to reach out with her arms for support. She stood up straight, then stumbled again as another wave hit and she went down into the water. Before Edward could reach her, someone else was lifting her from the water and struggling to drag her toward shore. Edward reached them while the water still lapped around their knees and together he and the stranger carried Edna's limp body to the dry sand and lay her down. A life guard raced toward them, and was checking for a pulse by the time the rest of the group got there.

"She's breathing," said the guard. "I don't think she took in any water. But she's out cold. Anyone know what the problem might be?" He was holding a cell phone. "Medics should be here in a few minutes. Does she have a history?"

"She's always been a strong swimmer. A mile nearly every day. But she's complained about getting tired easily since we've been here." Mattie's voice wavered and cracked, she sank to her knees and she began to sob. "Just blamed it on getting old. Edna! Edna. Can you hear me?"

Corinne knelt down with the blanket she had drug behind her as she ran. "It's not the O-word," she said. "Here — cover her — warm her up." The others looked at her quizzically.

"Do you know something we don't?" asked Mattie.

Corinne didn't answer. She knelt beside the inert form and began to run her fingers through Edna's hair, smoothing it back from the colorless face of her friend. "I told you not to go into the waves. I told you."

"Corinne — What is going on?" demanded Mattie. "What are you hiding from us?" She saw tears streaming down Corinne's face. She grabbed her by the shoulders and turned her to face them, and shouted, "What is the matter with Edna?"

Corinne forced the words out. "It's her heart. They told her not to swim any more till they could treat it. They didn't want her to come. She wouldn't listen — not to them and not to me." She turned back to her friend on the ground. "Oh, Edna, now look what you've done!"

Chapter 21

The five of them sat in the stark hospital waiting room together, a dozen straight-back chairs lining the walls.

"When did you know?" asked Mattie, not bothering to conceal her anger.

"Not until we were here," answered Corinne. "That first evening, when we were getting ready for bed, she handed me a form naming me as her medical power of attorney. Just in case, she said. But I pulled it out of her. Edna was never a 'just in case' sort of person. If she had taken the trouble to draw this paper up, there had to be a reason."

"You should have told me," said Mattie.

"She refused to let you know. You know how she can be. Didn't want to ruin the trip for you. She promised she wouldn't exert herself."

Julie had tears rolling down her cheeks. "Oh, God! Dear Edna! Corinne, how long has she been aware of this? Do you know how serious it is? Is she on medication?"

"From what she said — if she was being truthful — she went to the doctor a couple of weeks before we left. Routine check-up, she said, but he ran some tests, and didn't like what he saw. He wanted her to see a cardiac specialist, but she told him it would have to wait until after this trip." Corinne gripped the arms of her chair. "He wasn't happy.

Told her to be cautious, not to exert herself. They may have given her some medication, but I don't know. She did take some pills in the morning. She thought we wouldn't let her come if we knew — and of course, she was right about that."

"Stubborn Edna. Never listened to anyone. But she never put her life in danger for a silly trip before."

Julie reached out to touch Mattie's arm. "Is there anyone we should contact? Sisters? Brothers?"

"No one. She used our names — Corinne and I, for any emergency contact."

The door at the end of the room opened, and a doctor entered. He looked around at the group. His face was relaxed, but serious.

"Is one of you Corinne Thompson?"

"Yes," said Corinne, clutching the arms of her chair.

"I understand you are the patient's medical POA and that you have the papers." He sat down facing Corinne. His voice was warm and comforting. "I'm Doctor Phillips. Your friend is stabilized at the moment, and she is conscious. She's had a cardiac event. We aren't sure yet whether there was damage to the heart. We need to admit her to the cardiac unit while we run tests and decide how to proceed. We've sent word to her doctor in Phoenix, and are waiting for a reply. She's weak and confused. Can you give us permission to admit her, and run the necessary tests?"

"Of course. Whatever she needs," said Corinne, wiping her eyes. "When can we see her?"

He hesitated, then nodded his head. "I'll let you go in for five minutes. The rest of you will have to wait until she is settled in the unit, and then, only one visitor at a time." He stood up again and went to the door, then turned to face them again. "I know it must be hard to deal with a crisis so far away from home. She'll receive the best care possible. Be sure we have phone numbers where we can reach you twenty-four hours."

"We'll be right here," said Mattie. Corinne followed the doctor out of the room, and Mattie dropped her head to her hands. "Oh, why did I ever dream of such a stupid thing? Edna, Edna, Edna. What were you thinking?"

Julie reached out and took Mattie's hand. "She'll come through this, Mattie. I know she will. She has to."

Mattie squeezed Julie's hand, quietly stifling sobs. Edward put his arm around Julie. Robert sat silently lacing and unlacing his fingers. Minutes crawled by.

The door opened again and Corinne came in, her face pale and drawn. She dropped into the nearest chair, gripped her hands together, closed her eyes and nodded her head.

"Like the doctor said, she's weak and really confused. They have her hooked up to all kinds of monitors and tubes." She took a deep breath and looked around. "But she knew me, Mattie, and asked about you. Wanted to know if everyone else was okay, like we'd all been in an accident or something. She didn't seem to remember what happened."

"At least she could talk to you," said Julie.

"I had to lean close to hear, but she could talk."

"I need to see her," said Mattie, looking up and glaring at Corinne.

"They said they'd let us know when they had her moved, and you can see her then." Corinne reached for Mattie's hand, but Mattie jerked it away.

"I'm sorry, Mattie. She refused to let me tell you. I tried to keep her reined in. She knew what she was risking."

Mattie stood up, walked to the end of the room and pounded her fist against the wall. "I just feel so guilty for getting her into this."

Edward went to her and led her back to the chair next to Julie. "Mattie, you didn't get her into anything. You know Edna makes her own decisions. This one may have been unwise, but it was Edna's."

Julie hugged her aunt. "We've got to have faith, Aunt Mattie. I know she will be okay."

Two uncomfortable hours passed before a nurse finally came and took them to a more comfortably furnished waiting room in the cardiac unit. "One at a time," she reminded, and led Mattie into the patient area.

Mattie hardly recognized Edna. She was sunken into the pillow, looking half her usual size, tubes leading from her arm to bags suspended above her head, monitors beeping away, her face void of expression. Then recognition came into her eyes and the shadow of a smile.

"Edna, thank God you are okay." Mattie was choking back the tears as she leaned over and kissed Edna lightly on the cheek.

"Am I? Okay?" Edna whispered. "I'm sorry I scared you."

Mattie blinked back tears. "Sorry? I'm just glad you are still here, you silly goose. You just about scared us to death, but you're in good hands now, and you'll soon be good as new. Just rest now. Promise you'll be a good patient?"

Edna mouthed, "Sure."

"I won't scold you now. That can wait till we get back to Phoenix. Right now, you mind the doctor and the nurses. Get your strength back. We'll be right down the hall until you are out of here."

Edna seemed to revive a little. "I still don't know what happened. I really thought I was doing all right. Being careful. I felt fine. I'm sorry, Mattie. I'm sorry I messed things up. I should have stayed home. I was afraid you wouldn't go without me."

"You were right about that, but we could have done the trip later."

"Mattie." Edna lifted her hand slightly toward her friend. Mattie leaned closer. "Go sailing with Robert. Don't let Julie stop you."

Mattie was puzzled. "What are you talking about?"

"You owe it to yourself," said Edna.

Edward, Julie and Corinne each took a turn saying a few words to Edna, then they gathered in the waiting room again. It was getting dark outside; they were all tired.

"I'll stay here tonight," said Corinne. "If there is any change, if they need any permission, there won't be any delay."

"It's tomorrow that they'll be running tests, when the full staff will be here." said Edward. "I think that's when you might be needed, Corinne. I think you'd better try to get some sleep tonight."

"He's right," said Mattie. "I'll stay tonight. You'll only be a phone call away."

"None of you have had anything to eat," Robert spoke up. "The rest of you can get something at the house. I'll go get a sandwich or whatever Mattie would like and bring it to her. Hungry or not, you all need to keep your energy up."

They agreed and Corinne left with Julie and Edward. Robert followed.

Alone in the room, Mattie suddenly felt cold and weak. She leaned back in her chair, almost sobbing as she let out her breath. What would she do without her closest friend?

Chapter 22

Robert returned half an hour later with ham sandwiches, chips and iced tea. The first bite of food was hard for Mattie to get down, but then her appetite woke up, and she was thankful for the hearty sandwich and Robert's company.

"The three of you are very close," said Robert, unwrapping his sandwich.

"Yes. Edna and I were college roommates. Corinne just about saved Edna's life after a traumatic loss — just before my husband died. We've been through a lot together."

"I know it's too soon to know what you will need, but I'd like to help in any way I can. Housing, food, transportation."

"Thanks, Robert. We won't know, of course, until we get a diagnosis and treatment options. Angioplasty and we could be on our way home in a few days. Open heart and we could be here for quite a while."

"She was lucky at that. A minute earlier, while she was out just a little further, the waves would have rolled her under and she could've drowned before they got her out."

"I shudder to think how close it was."

A nurse came into the room with a blanket and pillows.

"I understand you will be staying the night. It's not the Hilton, but one of you will be pretty comfortable on that recliner. Will you both be staying? I can probably round up another reclining chair, though not as comfortable as that one."

"Just me," Mattie answered. "Be sure to let me know if anything changes."

"We will."

Robert shook his head when the nurse left the room. "I don't think she recognized me," he said. "She was a friend of my daughter's when they were in high school. I haven't seen her, or been in this hospital, since the night my wife died." He shook his head again and looked away. "Sorry," he said. "I shouldn't mention death when your friend is fighting for her life. Edna is in good hands. Top-notch staff here."

They finished the sandwiches, and Robert said tentatively, "I know how lonely this place can be. If you want company I could stay awhile longer. But sleep is what you need."

"Thanks. Thanks for everything you've done." Mattie realized she didn't want to be alone. "Your wife had a heart attack?"

"We knew she had some heart issues. She'd had angioplasty, we thought she was doing pretty good." He paused. "Then, one morning, she collapsed just after we'd started out to sea for the day. By the time I got the boat back to the dock, and the ambulance arrived, the damage had been done. She held on for a couple of days, but it was too late."

"I'm so sorry. Was it recent?"

"Ten years ago this month. But it seemed like yesterday when we came in here tonight."

"Some things don't go away."

"Yeah," he said quietly, clasping his hands together. Then he looked up at her again. "How did you all happen to make this trip?"

"Julie — she wanted to do something special for me — asked if there was anything on my bucket list I'd like to do." Mattie spoke slowly, remembering the conversation. "I'd never heard the term before. I told her no, that I had everything I wanted. She kept pushing me. There must be something I'd really like to do. I couldn't think of a thing."

"So why sailing? Was it something you thought about before?"

"Not consciously. I have a painting in my house. My husband, Jake, and I bought it on our last trip together. Nearly forty years ago." Mattie's eyes grew misty. "Anyway, I looked up at that picture. It's a sailboat. And suddenly, I knew I wanted to go sailing. I didn't even think about Julie's fear of boats at the time, though I guess I really should have. And here we are."

"You didn't really get much of a sailing experience."

"I was looking forward to getting on a smaller boat, but I enjoyed what I got. Can't have it exactly how we want things to be. If we have too clear a picture in our minds beforehand, nothing ever really measures up."

"You're right," he said.

"Right now, I just pray that Edna will be okay."

She leaned back in her chair again and closed her eyes, suddenly very tired. Robert stood up after a minute. He handed her the pillow, helped her recline the chair, and spread the blanket over her. He took her hand briefly, their eyes meeting.

"It gets chilly in here during the night," he said. "I hope you can sleep. Here is my phone number. Let me know if there is something I can do. I'll come around tomorrow again."

Chapter 23

There was no news about Edna during the night, and when Mattie questioned the woman at the nurse's station in the morning, she was told, "The doctor will be in soon."

Julie and Corinne arrived before eight o'clock, to find Mattie just folding her blanket. Edward had stopped at the cafeteria. Corinne went in to see Edna, leaving Julie and Mattie alone in the room.

"You probably didn't get any sleep at all," said Julie. "I didn't. Every time I closed my eyes, I just kept seeing Edna lying on the sand."

"I know," answered Mattie. "I'll never get that picture out of my mind either. What a nightmare this has become."

"Such a close call," said Julie. "I know we aren't out of the woods yet, but it's amazing that she didn't drown out there."

"I hope the doctor comes soon. Waiting, imagining the worst . . . But I can't let myself fall apart." Mattie was aware of tears on her cheeks. Julie moved to sit beside her aunt, and encircled her with her arms.

"She'll be okay, Mattie. Edna won't let this beat her." Julie reached for a tissue and gently wiped Mattie's eyes. "I know she'll be okay. Trust me. And all of you will be the wiser for the scare."

Corinne came back into the room. "She's much brighter this morning," she said. "More like herself. She's expecting you, but they're still saying one at a time."

Edna was propped up on pillows in the bed when Mattie entered the room. Color had returned to her skin, her hair was neatly smoothed around her face, and she smiled when she saw Mattie.

"How soon are they going to let me out of here?"

"Don't be so impatient, Edna. They don't even know for sure what the problem is yet."

"I feel so awful for ruining your trip." Edna looked down at the tubes going into her arm. "I should have stayed home."

"When did 'should' get so important to you?" asked Mattie, reaching for her hand.

Edna smiled wryly, looking up again. "Maybe I'll start listening to some of them. We are getting older, Mattie. I guess I still thought I was immortal."

"You scared us, Edna. Listen to the doctors here. I don't want to lose my best friend."

They waited anxiously for news, nibbling at the sweet rolls and boiled eggs Edward had brought to the waiting room. Finally, Dr. Phillips came in. He said Edna's coronary arteries were narrowed with plaque. He recommended immediate angioplasty treatment, which he had scheduled for the afternoon.

"She will be up and around tomorrow," he said, "but she will need to stay in the hospital a couple days while we make sure blood is flowing well and that there hasn't been serious damage to the heart muscle. Then it would be best if we can monitor her for a couple of weeks before she goes home."

The four conferred after the doctor left. They had two more days in the rental. Julie and Edward were both expected at work on Monday morning. Plane tickets for the three women would have to be changed. No matter if the doctors gave them clearance, they would not want to travel soon.

"We'll need a different place to stay," said Mattie. "This one is rented next week, and too expensive anyway."

Julie looked worried. "Everything is booked up so far in advance here. We may have trouble finding a place."

"I'll check with my travel agent in Phoenix," offered Corinne. "They probably have a branch here that could help us."

"We might ask the locals we've met if they have any suggestions," said Edward. "Robert, Charlie, Ruthie at the café. Maybe even the staff here at the hospital."

Robert walked into the room. They explained the situation to him.

"I can ask around my friends and neighbors," he offered. "Someone might know of a place available."

Mattie and Corinne were allowed in to see Edna together. Corinne repeated what the doctor had said, adding, "I'm so glad they can do it right away, Edna."

"But I feel fine now. It can't be that urgent."

"The doctor thinks it is," said Mattie.

"Surely it can wait till we get back to Phoenix. It will cost a fortune to stay longer." Edna's face grew tense, and she tried to sit up straighter. "Besides changing plane tickets."

"We'll just charge it all to your credit card!" said Mattie with a light laugh. "Won't hurt us a bit to have another two weeks of vacation."

By mid-afternoon, after a long anxious two hours in the surgery waiting room, the doctor came in and told them that the procedure had gone smoothly, but they would keep Edna in ICU overnight as a precaution.

When Mattie was allowed to see her again, Edna almost seemed like her old self. "Why can't we just fly home on Sunday as we had planned? Doctor Phillips says the problem should be taken care of, and I have doctors in Phoenix."

"Because Corinne and I aren't going anywhere with you for a while, even if the doctors said it was okay, which they have not. You're just going to have to be patient and listen to someone else for a while."

Chapter 24

"Mattie, doesn't this show you how crazy all this was? Edna should have been at home not nearly drowning herself in the ocean." Julie and Mattie were sitting across from each other in the waiting room.

"Julie, think of it this way. We should have been here, swimming and sailing, or climbing mountains somewhere, whatever we might have been tempted to do, for all these years. Yes, Edna should have told us about her condition, and we would have put off the trip until it was safe. But, you know," she grew pensive. "I'm not sure I wouldn't have done the same thing. And Corinne, too."

"Mattie!" Julie leaned forward and reached her hand out as if to stop what she was hearing. "How could you even think about throwing your life away?"

"A life not lived is a life thrown away, Julie." Their eyes locked. "Think about it. That's what the three of us were doing. Eating, breathing. Content, yes, not unhappy, but just waiting — for — what? We've enjoyed life more the past six months than we have in ten years. Planning." Mattie shook her head and stood up. "No, it wasn't just the planning. We were enjoying each day as it occurred. Life was fun again." She paced across the room, then turned back. "Memories are wonderful, Julie. I wouldn't give them up for the world. But they aren't particularly exciting, or satisfying. The past six months have been like a new life."

"And if this was too much for Edna? What if she doesn't make it?"

Mattie stopped, sat down again, and bit her lips. "I can't face that question right now," she said. "But Edna faced it, whether she came on this trip or not. She chose to make the most of the time left to her. Did she choose quality over quantity? We'll never know for sure. But Edna knew what her choice would be, no matter the outcome."

"I don't understand, Mattie. You always seemed happy."

"Happy is relative. I wasn't unhappy. And I don't expect to run around excited and dancing on the table all the time. But when every day starts to look and feel like every other one, well, you're in a rut and something needs to change. After we decided on this project, each day was a new day — even if I was going to do the same things I'd been doing for years. It just felt different."

"You can't expect to have something new and exciting in store every day, Mattie. Every day is every day. Just like every other day." Julie was beginning to pout.

"Have you ever felt like you were in a rut, Julie?"

Julie just looked at her blankly.

"No, I suppose you haven't. You were in school, then college, then you got married, and started working. And there are things you look forward to in the future. Promotions, buying a house, vacations." Mattie's voice became wistful. "A baby."

"Don't start the baby thing, Mattie. I've heard of mothers and mothers-in-law who pushed for a grandchild, but I never expected it from you. You chose not to have one yourself, so don't push me." Mattie was silent. She should never mention this. It was between Julie and Edward, and Mattie knew the two of them did not see eye-to-eye on the subject.

Julie continued, more softly. "We'll have a baby someday, Mattie. I'm just not ready yet. Edward knows how I feel."

"And you know how he feels?"

They turned away from each other as Edward and Corinne walked back into the room.

"I can help get you all settled in a new place," Edward was saying. "Provided we can find a new place. I'll need to fly home Sunday evening, but Julie can arrange to stay longer."

"I'll stay here, for sure," said Julie. "They can get along without me at work."

"This is Friday. We have the house until Sunday morning." Edward tapped his fingers as if counting off items. "Hopefully, they will keep Edna here until we are settled somewhere else. I'd like for the three of you to stay another two weeks before traveling with Edna. I want her to have a clean bill of health."

"My travel agent is talking to her colleague here," said Corinne, "but she says it won't be easy to find something on short notice. Even motels are booked up this time of year. And prices are sky-high."

"Something will turn up," said Mattie. "Think positive."

"Money is not an object," said Julie. "Just find the closest thing to the hospital, and eat meals out. Edward and I will handle the cost."

"Thanks, Julie, it's good to have your support. I told Edna it was all going on her credit card!"

"Mattie, Corinne," Julie said, holding her arms out as if to embrace them both. "I'd like you both to go to the cottage tonight and try to get a good night's rest," said Julie. "I will stay here. Neither of you look like you've slept in a week."

Edward intervened over their objections. "Julie's right. We all need to do our part to keep this ship sailing straight."

Chapter 25

Movement froze suddenly when Mattie's phone rang as they were eating breakfast at the cottage next morning. They all stiffened and stared at the phone, expecting bad news. Edward recovered first. "It's okay." he said. "If anything were wrong, Julie would call me first."

"You're right," agreed Mattie. "We're all just jumpy." She picked up the phone. "Hello?" It was Robert on the other end.

"Good morning," he said. "How are things going?"

"We're just finishing breakfast," she said. "We haven't heard anything from Julie yet. We'll be going to the hospital soon."

"I'm working on a couple of leads for housing. I think one of them might be just what you need. I'll meet you at the hospital and share what I find."

"Great! We'll be there in about half an hour. Come when you can." She lay the phone down and turned to the others. "Robert says he has a couple leads for us. He'll meet us at the hospital and tell us about it."

"Knowing someone local may make all the difference." said Corinne. "I'm so glad we got to know him."

They finished their meal and were getting into the car when Mattie's phone rang again. She picked it up.

"Hello, Mattie! This is Ruthie. I hope you don't mind that Robert gave me your phone number this morning. He told me about Edna's trouble. I wondered why he hadn't been in for a couple of days, or any of you. He said you are needing to find a different place to live, and I think I have a solution for you." She spoke rapidly. "My daughter has a vacation home here in Shelton. She rents it out occasionally, but keeps it pretty full with family and friends. It's empty now for a couple of weeks. She could let you have it for a nominal amount without the agency's fee. She's here now for the weekend, and would be glad to have you meet with her when you have time."

"Oh, Ruthie, that sounds wonderful," answered Mattie. "How's Edna this morning?"

"We're on our way to the hospital now. Julie said her spirits are better, and she's anxious to get out of the hospital. The doctor says she can be discharged on Sunday. That's the day we need to be out of our rental."

"I'll give you my daughter's phone number. Her name is Anita Brown. I told her to be expecting a call from you. Hope to see you for breakfast again soon. Gotta run now — I've got customers."

Mattie repeated Ruthie's message for the others. "Thank goodness," said Corinne. "Sure hope it works out."

"Ruthie's daughter's place would be perfect for you. It's right next to a small strip of beach," said Robert, when he arrived mid-morning. "The other option . . ." he hesitated. "You know — if finances are a problem, I have extra room at my place. I could let you have it, and Todd said I could bunk a few nights on his boat."

Julie was quick to jump in. "Edward and I will handle the expenses. We don't want to put anyone out. Corinne's travel agent may have found something by now."

"Thanks, that's a generous offer, Robert," said Corinne. "Let's call Ruthie's daughter and see how soon we can meet with her. We only have twenty-four hours to get a new place."

They made arrangements to meet Anita in an hour, and Robert drove them from the hospital. Just outside Shelton he pulled up to a slant-roofed saltbox style cottage at the edge of the road, overlooking the cove behind it. It wasn't far from where they were presently staying.

"Oh! We can still see the fishing pier!"

"Gorgeous! And the marina!"

"Beautiful!"

Anita greeted them at the door and showed them around. She was as warm and friendly as her mother. "I'll be leaving early tomorrow morning, before six," she said. "If you think this place will work, you can bring your things in as early as you wish."

There was a downstairs bedroom where Edna would be spared climbing stairs, and two more bedrooms on the second floor, with wonderful views of the ocean from the windows. At the back of the house, the kitchen opened onto a large outdoor porch with comfortable rockers, a swing and a barbeque. From the porch, a path led to a short flight of steps, and from there, down to a small, quiet beach. They settled with Anita on a reasonable price for two weeks.

"You will love the new place," Corinne announced when they were back at the hospital. Edna, sitting up in a chair, smiled wanly.

"I wish we could just call the whole thing off and be back home," she said.

"Now, Edna, don't be down about things," scolded Mattie. "We'll just make the most of these extra two weeks we've wound up with."

"We'll pretend it was part of the original plan, and have fun," said Corinne. "There are sunrises to watch, beaches to relax on, definitely another boat ride. And so much delicious food we haven't even sampled yet."

"We won't do anything strenuous," Julie said, reaching over to brush a lock of unruly hair back from Edna's face. "But Dr. Phillips said you could resume normal activity tomorrow, as long as you don't overdo it."

"The nurse had me walking up and down the hall all morning. I told her I wasn't training for a marathon."

"We'll pack your suitcase tonight for the move tomorrow. Anything you need us to bring to you here this afternoon?" asked Corinne.

"No," Edna replied. "They gave me a new toothbrush, comb and lotion. I sure don't feel ready for lipstick. And I don't feel like reading either. There's plenty to occupy my mind on the TV. In case I start to think too much."

Mattie and Corinne looked at each other and winced.

"Edna. You're going to be fine." Corinne said. "Not my thought — the doctor said so. Just take your medication, eat right, and do your exercises. We'll be back sunning on the beach in a couple of days. Check in with the cardiologist twice a week and we'll be home with a grand adventure under our belts, and no worse for the wear."

"Sure," Edna said. "I think I'm ready for a nap."

Julie spoke up now. "Why don't the three of you go home and start the packing? I'll stay here and make some phone calls for work — let my boss know the latest update. Where is that comb, Edna? I'll do your hair first, if you'd like. Then you can sleep awhile. I might even nap in this recliner myself."

Chapter 26

"You're looking so much better today," Julie said. She helped Edna sit up straighter, so she could reach her hair.

"I hope so," Edna replied. "They brought me a mirror yesterday and it scared me to death."

"Rightly so. You scared us all to death."

"I suppose you are going to scold me, too. Everyone else has."

"I hope they did a good job. You needed it," Julie teased. She ran the comb gently through the short, dark locks. "But, Edna, I was so afraid we would lose you. You mean so much to me — to all of us. Promise me you'll pay attention to the doctors from now on."

Edna smiled and nodded her head. "I suppose you're right. This time. But I was feeling fine. No symptoms of trouble. I just didn't think there was any hurry. And we were all having so much fun." Edna closed her eyes, and took a deep breath. "Anyway, everything is taken care of now. They say I can go home tomorrow."

"If only it was straight home — to Phoenix where you belong, where you are safe."

"Julie, it could have happened in Phoenix just as easily, you know. I could have been swimming at the Club. Or even just having dinner at the Wildebeest. These things don't always happen with exertion."

"Or you could have seen the cardiologist there and had treatment before anything happened at all. Like any sensible person would have done."

"Well, I guess 'sense' has never been one of my most prized possessions. But if I had always been sensible, I don't think life would have been near as much fun." Edna smiled and turned her head so she could look at Julie. "And we have had a lot of fun over the years, haven't we, Julie?"

"Oh, Edna, I was so frightened." Julie blinked back tears, and grasped Edna's hand. "I'm still frightened. I want this nightmare to be over. I want all of you back home safe in Phoenix."

Edna's face grew serious now, and she touched Julie's face. "You poor little girl. That's all you've wanted all your life, isn't it? For everyone to be safe, and where they should be. Especially Mattie. Maybe I tried too hard to show you how to have fun in spite of your fears. I didn't want you to be frightened of life, but maybe I did it all wrong."

"I'm not afraid of life, Edna," Julie protested. "It's losing people I love that frightens me."

"Losing those we love, in the end, is part of life. If you're afraid of dying, you're afraid of living. And life means living to the fullest — experiencing things. Having fun, yes, but experiencing all of it, the losses as well as the joys."

"I don't want to experience loss. It negates all the happiness."

"No, Julie. Loss hurts. I know it does. But it doesn't — we mustn't let it — negate the joy. Much of the joy we have in life is in our memories."

Julie laid the comb down. "When my parents died, they took all the memories with them."

"I don't think so, Julie. I think you buried them in your fears. I wish we had known then how important it was for you to keep your memories of them alive." Edna grasped Julie's hands, and drew her around so they faced each other. "But we didn't know, Julie. Nobody told us. We didn't know about the necessity of grieving. We wanted to protect you. So, we tiptoed around, trying not to mention your parents, because it upset you so much." Edna paused again. "I can see, now, how wrong we were. They were such vibrant, loving, and active people. They would have wanted you to remember them and all the things you did together when they were alive. Instead, you shut them up and all you remembered was the pain."

"I was so lost, Edna. So alone. Mattie was my life raft. She still is. You and her. I couldn't bear to lose either of you."

"Do you think you are the only one who knows about loss? I felt that way when Steven died."

"Mattie told me how lost you were. And about the baby. How Corinne helped you, and how long it took."

"Yes, it took a long time. Growing through a new friendship helped me recover. Walking with Mattie through the last months of Jake's life helped me to see that death is part of life." Edna paused. "Then you became part of Mattie's life, and we had a new task. To help you recover. Though we seem to have not completed that. We can't stop death, or loss. Our task is to grow through the losses, and preserve the happy memories."

"Do you really have happy memories of Steven and the baby?"

"Of Steven, yes — many. The baby — that's harder. But the love I felt for him, that is always with me, and I would not give it up in order to avoid the pain."

"My memories of Mommy and Daddy consist of their faces, with a red X across them. I have no happy memories."

"Really, Julie?" Edna's voice softened. "The Christmas we all spent together in Colorado, and your first ski lesson?" Julie gripped Edna's hands. Her eyes grew misty. "Your mother singing all your favorite songs while we sat on the patio watching the sunset?" Tears appeared on Julie's cheeks. "The day we went hiking on Camelback Mountain and your father had to carry you most of the way back? Don't you remember?"

Julie crumpled into Edna's arms, and sobbed.

Chapter 27

"She'll perk up when we get her out of the hospital and over to Anita's place," said Corinne, folding Edna's red sweater.

"I think so. I hope so," answered Mattie, opening the suitcase and laying it on the bed. "She wasn't herself at all today."

"Well, surgery, anesthesia, scaring herself, and everyone else, to death. Thank God it wasn't any worse." Corinne placed the sweater in the suitcase.

"If only she had told us. Even once we were here, if you had told us, we could have kept her away from the water."

Corinne turned to face her. "I couldn't, Mattie. She wouldn't let me. It would have been a betrayal."

"And betrayal to me that you held it from me."

"What would you have done, Mattie?"

"Oh, it's different between Edna and me. I would have stood up to her. You've always been more like a nursemaid to her."

"Or a sister. Mattie, don't let's fight about it. Edna knew what she was doing. I did what she wanted of me. She would never have forgiven me if I had told you. She gambled and almost lost. But she didn't lose. She's going to be fine."

"I hope so." Mattie turned and walked out of the room.

Edward stood in the kitchen, a half-filled box on the cabinet. He took a couple of cans from the cupboard and put them in the box.

"I guess we are through cooking in this place," he said, "but we'll use the rest of this stuff at the new place, starting tomorrow."

He looked at Mattie and saw the tension in her face. He stopped what he was doing, put his arm around her, and walked her to the couch.

"I know it was close, Mattie, but she's going to be fine."

"How could Corinne not have warned us?"

"I wondered the same thing at first," he said. "But friendships each have their own boundaries. Edna told Corinne — instead of you — because she knew where those boundaries were between them. She didn't want us to know. It wasn't Corinne, it was Edna who made that decision."

"Oh, Edward, I'm so mixed up inside. So thankful she's okay, so angry with them both, wondering how I could have been so self-centered that I didn't notice all Corinne's cautions. *Better not climb the stairs, Edna. You look tired, Edna. I think you should take a rest before we go. What's wrong, Edna?* Corinne may have a motherly side, but she was beginning to sound like Julie. I should have noticed."

"Don't blame yourself. Julie and I didn't notice either. We just weren't looking for trouble."

"Years ago — we were just out of college — someone said 'Always look for trouble when you are with Edna.' But I never felt that way. I always felt safe with her. I thought she was the wise one, the strong one of my friends. I guess I thought she would be here when everyone else was gone." They were silent for a minute, then Mattie continued. "But when she broke down, it was Corinne and Art who pulled her up to her feet. Jake and I couldn't do it."

Corinne came out of the bedroom, pulling Edna's suitcase. "Her clothes are all packed. I'll put the rest of her stuff in the carry-on." She put the suitcase near the door. "Maybe you should go back with Julie. I think I'll take a nap before I do my own stuff."

Edward walked back into the kitchen and opened the refrigerator. "You know, we never cooked that swordfish we bought on Wednesday afternoon. I wonder if it's still good? If it is, we'd better cook it."

"It's okay. I put it in the freezer when we got up that morning," said Corinne, "not knowing when we'd be ready to cook again. We can thaw it tomorrow, and Edna will be ready for a home cooked meal."

Mattie agreed. "But let's do cook here tonight. We can use up the eggs and make some waffles with that marvelous waffle maker we haven't used yet. It will do us good to be busy here, and Edna doesn't need all four of us standing around watching her like vultures."

"You're right," said Corinne, "but I'm still going to have that nap. It's only 3 o'clock. I'll be up in time to help with the cooking."

"I'll get my suitcase packed," said Edward, "then go back over to the hospital. Julie can come back and help with the cooking, or at least enjoy the food. Actually, Edna might like being alone for a little while. You are right about us standing around, expecting her to wilt any minute."

While Corinne napped and Edward headed back to the hospital, Mattie stepped out onto the porch. She sat down and looked out over the street, across the swell of sea grass and down to the little beach. She could hear the soft murmur of the waves moving gently against the sand. A family was wading, and preparing to grill on the beach. A couple of sail boats glided past each other, and a motor boat moved quickly farther out on the water.

How peaceful it looked, Mattie mused. Not like her own thoughts. She almost resented the quiet, tranquil scene in front of her. It had seemed so perfect before. Now it was like a challenge. She thought back to those exciting, happy hours in Phoenix while they planned their great escape. How long had Edna known? Only a week or so Corinne had said, but who knows for sure with Edna?

Mattie's mood brightened instantly as she saw Robert's familiar blue car turn off the road and park at the side of the house.

"I didn't want to block your view," he said as he came up to the porch.

"And what a great view it is." Mattie smiled and held her hand out to him.

He squeezed it briefly, then sat down in the chair next to her. "How is Edna?"

"Her spirits were down a bit today. Unusual for Edna. But it's hard to change her once she gets in a mood. When we get her to Anita's house, she'll start looking up again. It would be hard to feel depressed in that house, I think. We're so thankful you found it for us, Robert."

"I was thinking about stopping at the hospital this evening and saying hello to her. Do you think she would mind?"

"Of course not. She'd love to see you."

"She had a close call. Why did she take the chance?"

"Edna doesn't let much slow her down when she gets something in her mind." She paused. "We were in a rut. Had been for fifteen years. Once we got the idea — thanks to

Julie and her bucket list — we were all really excited. Realized we didn't need to sit in our rocking chairs all day just because we were now senior citizens by anyone's standard." Her voice grew quiet and she gazed out at the water. "Seems as if we almost waited too long."

He nodded, following her gaze. "I guess that pier has been my rocking chair since Mary died." He was silent for a moment, then he turned toward her. "Mattie, meeting you folks has woken up something in me, too. Made me look forward to — I don't know what. Just living day to day can be more than sitting on the pier watching the boats come in and out."

She met his eyes just for a moment, then looked down at her hands. "What happened makes me realize that we shouldn't wait if there is something we want to do," she said. "There may not be much time at all." They were both silent for a moment before Robert replied.

"Strange, but I remember feeling that way when I was much younger." His voice was soft. "It seemed there was all the time in the world, yet we didn't want to waste any of it. As we got older, and actually had less time in front of us, we let it slip away faster, without thinking about it." He turned to her, took a deep breath, and said quickly, "I'll have my boat back by the end of next week, Mattie. I'd like to take you out for a day."

"That would be wonderful, Robert," she said, meeting his eyes again. "Sounds even better than going with Todd." Suddenly, she felt self-conscious under his gaze. Standing up quickly, she gestured toward the house. "Can you stay this evening for eggs and waffles? We need to eat up some groceries instead of moving them."

They were busy together in the kitchen when Julie arrived a short time later. She looked at them with a glint in her eyes, but greeted them pleasantly.

"Edward said we are having eggs and waffles, so I stopped at the store and picked up syrup. Just a small bottle. One more thing to move I guess, if we don't use it up. I didn't know you were joining us, Robert."

"He stopped by to ask about Edna and I invited him to help us eat up the food. And there is still a little of that ham. It will taste good after cafeteria food for two days — even if they did have a pretty good menu."

Corinne joined them in a few minutes.

"Smells good out here," she said, lifting the lid of the frying pan where the ham was sizzling.

"Ready to drop the eggs into the skillet when the waffles are cooking," Julie said as she set plates around the table. "That double Belgian waffle maker will make enough so that we can all start together. By the time we've each eaten half of one, the next batch will be ready."

After dinner, Robert excused himself to go see Edna. "I can give Edward a ride home so you won't have to go back," he said to Julie.

"I'd like to go back too," said Corinne. "We'll take both cars, in case I want to stay a little longer. I still feel bad to have Edna there by herself at night."

"She's being released in the morning," Julie reminded her. "Then maybe we can get a normal routine going again."

Julie and Mattie went to sit on the porch when they left.

"Now do you see, Mattie? You aren't young anymore. You are putting your lives in danger."

"Don't start, again, Julie. I'm worried sick about Edna. I don't need another lecture from you about rocking chairs.

You aren't worried about life. You are worried about death. To me, and to Edna, life is a lot more important than death."

"She could have died out there. Then what would her life have been like?"

"It would have been a beautiful life, lived as fully as she knew how. She made some choices when she came here with us. Maybe they were foolish, but I will defend her right to make those choices. But she didn't die, Julie. She gambled and won — at least temporarily."

"Temporarily!! Mattie, how can you think it's okay to risk her life?"

"Julie, you risk your life every day in one way or another."

"Those are the risks of everyday living. You can't live without getting in a car. But you don't need to take risks for nothing."

"And pleasure? Freedom? Joy? Are these nothing, Julie?"

"Nothing compared to losing your life, leaving those who love you to grieve when they might not have had to."

"Is that it, Julie? Edna should have curtailed her own desires to save you and me and Corinne the possibility of grief? Surely you don't believe that?"

Chapter 28

"Look, Edna! The view is gorgeous, and from the back porch, we can walk right down to the beach." Mattie swept her outstretched arms across the panoramic view, as Edward helped Edna from the car.

Edna looked at the house then gazed out over the cove. "You're absolutely right," she said. "It is beautiful. Though not any prettier than where we were. I'm glad you were able to find something — thanks to Robert, I understand. And Ruthie."

Julie came out of the door, skipping down the steps to greet Edna with a warm hug. "Welcome home. It is so good to have you back with us."

Corinne was right behind her, wiping her hands on her apron. "I won't hug you right now. I've got swordfish on my hands. Getting it ready for the grill."

"Swordfish? Haven't you eaten that yet? I think it's a bit old by now."

"No, luckily Corinne thought to freeze it, and we just took it out to thaw this morning. Robert says it's his favorite fish of all," Mattie said "so we've invited him over to cook it for us. We'll eat early so Edward won't miss out. The shuttle is coming to take him to the airport."

They moved into the house, and showed Edna around. By the time Robert arrived, the barbeque was lit, fresh vegetables were on skewers and corn on the cob was husked. Before long, the swordfish was grilled perfectly.

After the meal, Julie and Edward volunteered for kitchen clean-up and left the others relaxing on the porch.

"I'll talk to you every day, Julie," Edward told her, "and if I need to come back, it doesn't take long to get here. If they don't re-route the plane through Newark again. I never quite figured that one out. You have a board meeting on Thursday?"

"I don't think I'll come home for it," said Julie. "I'm uneasy about leaving them here, especially with that man hovering around. I'll be so glad when they are safely back in Phoenix and things are normal again."

"Oh, stop that nonsense about Robert." Edward scowled at her. "He is a perfect gentleman, and I feel a lot more comfortable knowing that someone who knows his way around the area is looking out for them. He has my phone number, and will let me know if anything seems amiss."

"I don't like the way he looks at Mattie."

"How is that?"

"You know. Just — too interested. Too ready to help. Answering every question. Offering to let us stay at his place, or give us a ride on his sailboat if it were here."

Edward stopped what he was doing, turned and cupped his hands gently on his wife's shoulders. "What are you afraid of, Julie? Are you afraid that she might be — interested? And what if she were interested — in Robert, or someone back in Phoenix? Do you want her all to yourself? Forever? Isn't thirty years long enough? Maybe she wants her life back, Julie. Did you ever think of that — how much of her life she gave up for you?"

Julie stepped back, pushing him forcefully away. She raised her voice. "How dare you! You know I love Mattie more than anything. I don't demand all her time. She has Edna and Corinne. I'd do anything for her. If someone hurt her, I'd kill them. If Robert so much as touches her . . ."

"Julie, some things are not your decisions to make."

"What are you implying? She's seventy years old, for God's sake. She's old. And vulnerable. Gullible even. What does she know about what goes on in the minds of old men?"

"Apparently more than you do, my dear."

Their voices had reached a crescendo, and they stepped back, glaring at each other. Edwards final remark was heard clearly on the veranda, as the music had stopped at that precise moment. Julie ran to the stairs, leaving Edward to hang up the tea towel and join the others outside.

Chapter 29

"Take care of my harem for me," said Edward grasping Robert's hand as Charlie's shuttle stopped in front of the house.

"I'll try," answered Robert, "but I think that might be a tough job."

Edward gave each of the woman a hug, including a warm kiss for Julie, and got in the vehicle. They all stood watching it disappear around the corner.

"Do you think it would be okay to walk down and sit on the beach for a while?" asked Edna. "I feel a little stir-crazy."

Mattie looked at her hesitantly.

"They said to resume normal activity, so I don't know why not. They've had you all over the halls in the hospital," said Corinne. "I'll bring a chair for you. Everyone coming?"

The gentle breeze was pungent with the ocean air. They set the beach chairs where the sand was dry and watched the waves lap against the shore, and wondered aloud what plans they should make for the coming week.

"We've certainly had excitement enough to last for a long time," said Julie. "There is a whole wall shelved with books in the living room. I want to pick one and curl up somewhere and just read all day."

"Breakfast — or at least brunch — at Ruthie's again," voted Edna. "Tomorrow would not be too soon."

"Early enough to watch the sunrise," added Corinne.

"With an umbrella for shade, I could probably sit right here all day," said Mattie.

"Except that 'right here' gets pretty wet when the tide comes in," said Robert, smiling. "Tell you what. I live just about a stone's throw from here. I usually get to Ruthie's just before sunrise. That's about 5:30. I'll come by about 5:00 and anyone who is up and waiting on the porch can jump in with me. I won't wake you — you'll have to be up and ready."

"We have the car. We can drive when we are ready," said Julie shortly. "There's no need for you to come by."

"Just an offer," he said. After a moment of silence, Edna and Corinne continued to make suggestions.

"Another of those wonderful Margaritas, where we sat watching those huge waves against the rocks that night. Is it all right for you to have a drink, Edna?"

"I asked about a glass of wine, and the doctor said that was okay, so I guess so. They really didn't give me any restrictions, except not to over-do."

"We never got to that aquarium. How far is that, Robert?"

"About a forty-minute drive. Takes about an hour to walk through, though if you find it interesting to watch the tidepools and sea creatures and the videos they have available, you can spend most of the day. I took my grandson last year, and he didn't want to come home at all. It was a wonderful way to spend the day with him. I learned a lot myself."

It was beginning to get dark before they folded their chairs and began making their way back to the house. Robert gave Edna his arm, carrying both their chairs in the other hand. It was a gentle rise except for the seven or eight stairs at the edge of the sand.

"Didn't even tire me," declared Edna as she reached the top of the steps. "I feel better than I did before."

Back at the house, Robert replaced the chairs in the cupboard, and then said, "Well, I guess I'll say good night, ladies."

Mattie stepped toward him. "About breakfast," she said. "Why don't you come on by at five? I'd really like to see the sunrise. If we are all up, we can follow you, but if not, I'd love to ride in before the others. They can meet us at the café." She smiled at Robert, and kept her eyes resolutely away from Julie.

Robert looked vaguely uncomfortable for a moment, then grinned broadly. "Sure thing, Mattie. Any of you that want to go early. Ruthie has the grill going by 6:00. Coffee even earlier." As he got in his car, he turned and waved to them again and the women waved in return.

"Really, Mattie, we don't have to impose." Julie's voice was tight.

"I never saw anyone look less imposed on," said Edna. "What a friend he has turned out to be!" She turned and entered the house, followed by Corinne, leaving Julie and Mattie glaring at each other. After a moment, Julie let out a sigh and followed them.

Mattie was not ready for sleep. She stayed in the chair on the porch, and watched the moonlight glistening on the water. She had surprised herself by challenging Julie. But it had seemed important that she speak up. Why did Julie resent Robert so much? Almost as much as Mattie was beginning to resent Julie.

After a while, Edna came out of the house, dressed in her pajamas, holding two small wine glasses. "Bravo, Mattie," she said, handing one glass to Mattie and holding up the other one as if for a toast.

"What is happening to us, Edna?" said Mattie, taking the glass. "I feel like Julie is choking me, like she is trying to put me in a box with a lid."

"Well, don't let her do it," Edna said, sitting down. She pulled a light blanket from the back of the chair and pulled it around her. After a while, she said, "You know, Mattie, in a way, she's had you in a box for years, though it seemed the lid was left open. Now that she sees you could climb out, she's frightened."

"Of what? It's not like I have any active part in her daily life. I live two thousand miles away; she doesn't even know what I do at home. What does it matter if I take a trip, do something different? What is she afraid of?"

"In her mind, she thinks she's protecting you." Edna swirled her glass. "But I think she really sees Robert as a potential escape hatch."

"Ridiculous."

"Is it, Mattie? It's been a long time since I've seen you look at a man as if — well — as if he were a man."

"Oh, Edna!" Mattie tossed her head. "You're imagining things. We've all found a friend in Robert."

Edna laughed and stood up as abruptly as she had sat down. "Enjoy your breakfast in the morning, Mattie. I'll keep Julie here, somehow." She raised her glass toward Mattie again, and went back into the house.

Chapter 30

"No one else is up yet," Mattie said as she got in Robert's car the next morning. "Edna was supposed to set the alarm, but she just got up a minute ago."

"Should we wait?"

"No, she said for me to go on ahead." Mattie felt a little guilty, but Edna had shooed her out the door.

As they pulled into the small parking area, Mattie said, "I think I'd like to watch the sunrise from the pier. Is that okay? Will I scare the fish?"

"Hard to scare ocean fish," Robert replied. "We'll borrow one of Ruthie's deck chairs so you have something to sit on." They walked almost to the end of the pier before Robert put down his gear and the chair, and got his line out into the water. He poured coffee from a thermos into two mugs.

There were no clouds for the sunrise to paint with pinks and oranges. "The sun just sort of pops up all at once on clear mornings like these," he said. "It takes at least a few clouds for the really pretty skies."

"It's like that in Phoenix too," she answered. "But we usually have a haze at least in the evening."

"I found this spot, here at the end of this dock, after Mary died, and I spent most of the next six months here. It was lonely."

"That was what took the longest for me, after Jake died. The loneliness. It just seemed to get worse, day after day, month after month." She blew across the top of the mug of hot coffee. "Then a couple years later, Julie came to me. That changed everything. I wish Julie and Edward would have a baby. Maybe she wouldn't worry about me so much then!"

Robert laughed. "She is a bit like an over-protective mother, isn't she? I thought she was your granddaughter at first. You didn't have children of your own?"

"No. I've often wished that I'd had a child with Jake. We knew we only had a few years together, and I was frightened at the thought of raising a child by myself. As it turned out, raising Julie was a blessing to me, even though losing my sister was terrible."

"It must have been awfully hard to lose your husband so young."

"It was hard, but I'm sure it wouldn't have been any easier after another 20 years."

"Never wanted to remarry?" He deftly flicked the fishing line out further, keeping his eyes on it.

"Never really explored that possibility," she said. "Without Julie, it might have been different. I put all my energy into trying to be a mother to her."

"I don't envy the thought of single parenting. The kids kept us busy enough for three or four hands. It's tough sometimes, being a parent, but there's a lot of joy."

"I suspect that Julie thinks I chose sailing as a way to challenge her, but I really didn't even think at all before I said it. I just looked up at that picture, and it popped into my head and out of my mouth."

"The picture you'd bought with your husband?"

"It was our last trip together. We knew there wasn't much time left. I'm not sure why the painting meant so much to us. The sailboat seems to be coming in toward — or going away from — a pier like this one. I was never sure which, it seemed to change day by day. But since the day it suggested this trip, it has seemed like it was bringing a gift to me."

Mattie was gazing out over the breakers. Robert watched his line in the water intently.

Finally, he said, "Well, Mattie, when I have my boat back next week, we'll see if that was right."

After a minute, he moved closer to her chair and handed the fishing pole to her. He placed her hands carefully on the pole. "See? Like this," he said, covering her hands with his own for a moment. Shivers ran up Mattie's spine, and she kept her eyes on the spot where the fishing line entered the water.

"If a fish strikes, you might lose your pole when it pulls it out of my hands," she said, with a short laugh.

"It will pull the line out first," he said. "I'm ready to grab and help." He refreshed the coffee in their mugs. They sat silently for a while, an unfamiliar tension between them. Finally, he reeled the line in and secured the hook.

"I think it's time for our breakfast," he said. "The fish are sleeping in today."

They greeted Ruthie and as they made their way to a table on the deck, the other women arrived and joined them. They decided together that they would like to spend most of the day at home, then go out to dinner. Tomorrow they thought would be a good day for a trip to the aquarium.

"Will you join us tomorrow, Robert?" asked Corinne.

"Glad to," he said. "Shall I plan to drive?"

"That would be great, we won't get lost on the way then. The directions sounded a little confusing."

"It isn't really hard to find, but there are a couple of turns that are easy to miss."

They lingered long into the morning over their breakfasts and endless cups of tea and coffee. They reminisced about their adventures from the week before. Edna said she would still like to go whale watching. "That shouldn't be too strenuous."

"The museum had all sorts of pictures, models, and even videos of them," said Julie. "I'll take my whales second hand, thank you! Will they have anything like that at the aquarium?"

"No, it isn't designed for show. They have a couple of rescued seals, but they do not perform."

Ruthie came to the table with a fresh pot of coffee. "If you are looking for something to do this weekend, remember the festival downtown. Artists, entertainers, dancing on the boardwalk 'til midnight. They have a chowder cook-off that guarantees the best seafood chowders on the coast. Have you told them about that, Robert?"

"No, I guess I had sort of forgotten. The ladies were not planning on being here that long."

"I love any kind of festival," said Corinne. "What's the theme?"

"It celebrates the founding of our town," said Ruthie. "We aren't as old as some of the ports around here, but we are pretty proud of our heritage. Robert's wife, Mary, was a direct descendent of the first mayor."

"It was a pretty important event to her. We always got involved in the planning. Since her passing, I've just stood back and watched, I guess."

"They're expecting rain this week," said Ruthie. "It isn't supposed to be a major storm, though, and should clear up by the weekend. At least we hope so."

Boats skimmed across the water in the cove in front of them. Sails moved past smoothly, while motor boats kicked up a wake behind them. Several fishermen lined the pier.

"There have been times when the waves have broken over the pier, but it takes a pretty powerful storm to do it," said Robert. "It's an impressive sight when it happens. It will wreak havoc even on the boats at dock in the harbor. The hurricane a couple years ago almost washed the pilings out from under this deck. The beach in front of your house was formed then, while the one down where you were staying was re-configured completely. Washed most of the sand away, exposing those big rocks."

"I suppose you've been caught in a storm now and then when you were out sailing?" said Corinne.

"I'm not much of an adventurer, but there have been times when I wished I'd stayed in port for the day," he laughed. "Of course, it wouldn't be much fun to sail in a bathtub either. I never courted danger, but you do want to feel the wind and water against the boat and your sail. I always thought the speedboat guys were trying to make their own wind and current, controlling it themselves. In a sailboat you don't control the waves and the wind, you just try to control the boat, help the boat survive in them."

"And sometimes they don't." Julie's voice was calm, but her eyes seemed to glare at Robert.

"You're right, Julie." He nodded his head. "There is an inherent risk. Just as there is every time you get in a car."

"That's different. You have to live in the world today. But most of us do not have to get in a boat."

"You didn't have to ride that roller coaster last summer either," said Corinne. "But you sure seemed to enjoy it."

Julie's jaw was tight. She looked from one of her companions to the other, blinked her eyes and abruptly got up and walked to the far end of the deck.

Mattie followed her. She placed her hand on Julie's shoulder.

"Julie. There have been literally hundreds of boats out there while we've been here and not one of them has gotten in trouble."

There were tears on Julie's eyes when she turned to face Mattie. "You aren't on any of them, Mattie. I'm so afraid for you. Please don't — just please don't . . ."

Mattie put her arms around her and embraced her. "Oh, Julie, bless your heart." After a moment, she led Julie back to the table. "Let's have some of Ruthie's pastry," she said, and went inside to order.

Chapter 31

"You and Edna set it up between you, didn't you?" Julie and Mattie were alone on the porch in the afternoon. Edna and Corinne were napping.

"What do you mean?"

"Edna forgot to set the alarm on purpose — just so you could be alone with that man."

"He has a name, Julie."

"What are you looking for, Mattie?"

"What are you afraid of, Julie?"

Julie's clenched fists were shaking as she raised them to her chin.

"Afraid? Yes, I am afraid. He isn't Robert Redford, Mattie. He's — he's — I don't know what he is, or what he's looking for, and I don't care. It's you I care about."

"Is it? Is it really? Or do you just want to keep your own little world snug and safe in a bottle? You and Edward just as you are. No changes to anything, ever, from here on. Me, safe and snug in Phoenix where I belong. You know it can't be like that forever, Julie."

"What's between Edward and me is just between us, Mattie. We don't need your advice."

"And my life is for me to determine. I don't need you to make my decisions, Julie."

"And your decision making almost killed Edna."

"You are the one who suggested a bucket list! Well, swimming in the ocean again was at the top of Edna's list! She took a chance, Julie, a chance to do something she really wanted. Did you ever take a chance at something you really wanted? Is anything worth taking a chance to you? Is there anything you want out of life besides being safe in your tight little box?" Mattie was surprised by her own sudden, bitter anger toward Julie.

In turn, Julie stared in disbelief at her aunt. "I don't know what this conversation is about any more, Mattie. Yes, I want you safe. Why would I want anything to change? I love you. I love Edward. And Edna and Corinne too. I don't want anything to change."

"But things will change, Julie." Mattie held her hands out toward Julie, pleading. "Eventually it will all change. Even you. What will you do then? Don't you understand?"

"I understand that you're not yourself anymore." Julie stood up and walked to the edge of the porch. "Not since this whole thing started."

Mattie's voice became soft, and she spoke slowly. "Maybe I was never the person you thought I was," she said. "Maybe you made up who you thought I was. And maybe I played the part without realizing it. But, Julie, I feel more like myself than I have in years. And Edna and Corinne feel it too." Julie leaned against the porch railing, staring at Mattie, and shook her head. Mattie continued, "But you are right. Edna kept you here this morning, but not just so I could be alone with Robert. She did it because she wanted to open the box she thought you had put me in, and she wanted me to escape. I'm not sure what I want, Julie. But I want to see outside the box. I want to set my own boundaries. And maybe I want to get to know Robert a little better. Is that so threatening to you?"

Julie sobbed once, then she turned and ran into the house.

There. She had said it. And she couldn't un-say it. She wanted to get to know Robert a little better. Friendly curiosity. That's what it was. He was such a nice man. So thoughtful. Obviously he enjoyed their company.

Why shouldn't they all get better acquainted?

Mattie sank down into the porch chair. Julie was suffocating her. How long had this been happening without her recognizing it? Why, at seventy years of age, did she suddenly feel like running away from home? What home, for heaven's sake? There was no one to run away from. What was she thinking?

She let herself lean back into the chair, turning her face up toward the sun, her eyes closed. Thoughts in turmoil. Anger, confusion, fear, determination. Julie, looking so hurt, fighting with Edward. Edna falling beneath the water, lying still on the sand. Corinne, tears streaming down her face. Anger at them all, fear for them all. Guilt for getting them all into this mess.

Slowly her mind slowed, and she began to separate different threads. Edna, independent, determined as she had always been. Yes, the decision to put off the visit to the cardiologist until after the trip was consistent with her nature. And Edward had been right about why she had confided in Corinne rather than her. And of course Corinne was right in keeping her confidence. I'm just so thankful Edna is okay. But I owe Corinne an apology.

But Julie. That was a different matter. What in the world was happening between them? It was more than the boat. Mattie knew that now. And whatever it was, it's affecting Julie and Edward as well.

The women cooked dinner at home that night. There was tension in the air, but conversation was light and without conflict.

They took their beach chairs down to the sand after they finished eating. The water lapped close to their blanket, but it was receding. There were a few boats still on the water. The sky was clear. The friends were silent.

Mattie thought about how exciting the trip had seemed from Phoenix, and how little it had measured up. The sail boat ride she had conjured in her mind had not happened. Though she enjoyed the ride that first day with Todd, it wasn't what she'd had in mind. She and Julie seemed more estranged every day. Edna and Corinne both seemed quiet and subdued.

She looked over at Edna, who leaned back in her chair with her eyes closed. She looked drawn and tired.

"Are you okay, Edna?"

Edna snapped her eyes open and turned to look at Mattie. "Yes. I'm okay. Are you going to treat me like an invalid the rest of my life? Can't I close my eyes without everyone panicking?"

"I'm sorry, Edna."

Corinne broke the stiff silence that followed. "Shall we take one of those evening cruises tomorrow evening?"

"Don't forget we've planned the aquarium tomorrow," said Julie. "We can do the cruise on Wednesday if the weather holds."

"What would you do while we are on the boat?"

Julie was silent for a minute. "I suppose — well, sailing is what we came for, isn't it? I suppose I could come along. I'm not sure if Edward will be back by then."

They all looked at her, surprised.

Edna sat up. "That would be great, Julie, if you are up to it."

"I don't want to be a weight you're dragging behind you."

"Then we'll do one just for you, Julie," said Corinne. "There's the cranberry bog, the Sandwich Glass museum, potato chip factory, or all sorts of touring. We haven't even seen half of the villages yet, and none of us has purchased a souvenir."

"Julie, you should look through all the brochures and literature I've collected at every stop we've made, and decide what you would most like to do."

"The festival this weekend that Ruthie mentioned would be fun," said Julie. "And there're music concerts in some of the local areas. Not everything happens on a boat."

"We could rest and relax most of the day on Wednesday," said Mattie. "Though maybe it would be better to keep you busy so you won't be worrying about the boat ride all day."

"There is a lot to see in Woods Hole tomorrow besides the aquarium."

They turned in early that evening. It had seemed like a long day, even though relaxing.

Julie tossed restlessly on the bed, as she listened to the murmur of the waves through the open window. She wished Edward were with her. She was frightened. She wanted to turn the calendar back six months. She wanted Mattie to be the old Mattie she had relied on for so many years. Her rock, her point of comfort.

Was she clinging too tightly? Edward had asked the same questions as Edna. And now Mattie herself had said she felt she was being kept in a box. But it was a safe box, wasn't it? Wasn't safety important?

What could be missing from Mattie's life? She had a nice home, friends, and adequate income. If she wanted a change she could come and spend some time with Julie and Edward. They'd invited her often, though she had only come once in the five years of their marriage.

Why, suddenly, did Mattie want change, adventure? What had made the painting come to life that day? It was vivid in Julie's mind. The fishing pier stretching out into the water, just like the one by Ruthie's café. The sailboat moving gently on the water. The man sitting at the end of the pier.

The man turned around in her mind, and Julie saw Robert smiling at her.

She sat up in bed, suddenly choking with fear. "No!" she cried out loud. She held her hands to her head, her breath coming in gasps. She threw back the sheet, stood up, and stumbled to the window.

"Mattie," she whispered. "I love you."

Chapter 32

The next morning, Mattie slept late for the first time since they had arrived on the Cape. When she woke up, she found Corinne and Julie in the kitchen with sweet rolls and sausage and fresh strawberries set out.

Julie greeted her with a quick hug. "Grab a plate and come out to the porch. You'll need a sweater, it's cool this morning, but the air is fresh and invigorating. A nice breeze."

Julie carried the coffee pot out onto the porch with a tray of cups, while Mattie and Corinne each carried a plate of food.

"Robert will be here soon," said Mattie. "I'm glad he'll be driving."

"Where is Edna this morning?"

"She said she never intends to get up in a hurry again in her life," answered Corinne. "That she was going to take all the time she wanted to do up her face and fix her hair. Said she was going to pretend she was a princess and everyone could just wait on her."

Julie and Mattie laughed. "So what's new?" asked Mattie. "She always thought she was a princess."

"She has a point," said Julie. "We should all have a new appreciation for time and its limitations after the past few days."

"Strange how our sense of time changes," observed Mattie. "When we have lots of it stretching out in front of us, we want to fill every minute with activity. There is so much to be done and we want to do all of it. Then, we get older, and actually have less time to do all the things we want. Then we try to slow it down, and take our time to do things slowly, as if there is no rush at all. I think we have it backwards, sometimes."

"We all need a bucket list to help us set priorities and work to accomplish what we want," said Corinne.

Edna came out of the house with a smile on her face. "Strange. I think I feel better than I have in months. Maybe years."

Mattie smiled. "Well, getting some blood and oxygen to your brain and muscles might have that effect, now that I think of it. From what the doctor said, it's a wonder you didn't collapse long before you did."

Edna poured herself a cup of coffee and sat down. "Immortality suffered a blow, but I guess I survived. By the way, have any of you been to the doctor lately? At least I've had a checkup every two years."

"Mine's due next month," said Mattie.

"Every August, around my birthday," said Corinne.

They looked at Julie. "The latest guidelines I read said yearly checkups are not necessary and may even do more harm than good." She shrugged her shoulders. "So many tests lead to false positives. It's gotten to be a problem."

Edna turned to face her. "Strange philosophy for someone who seems more afraid of death than any of us."

"Well, I mean, you can't spend all your time thinking about it."

"Unless it's about someone else? You shouldn't worry about yourself, but it's okay to be paranoid about those around you?"

"The more we talk the more confused I get," said Julie. "Are you all making fun of me?"

"No, Julie," said Corinne. "At least we don't mean to. Maybe it's just the generation gap."

"Here's Robert," said Mattie, as he came around the corner of the porch. "Are we all ready?"

"Shall we take sandwiches, or eat out?" asked Corinne.

"Eat out. I want to find the smallest little hole in the wall café that has never heard of a tourist. Is there such a place on Cape Cod, Robert?"

"Probably not, Edna. People don't come here to get away from it all. They come wanting to see what the fuss is all about. It is a different place than when I was growing up, but it still has its beaches, its scenery. And a few quiet places, if you know where to look."

"You know," said Edna. "After today, I wouldn't mind if we spent the rest of our time just sitting here looking over the water. I think I've had enough adventure."

"But Mattie hasn't had her sailboat ride yet," said Corinne. "We'd better call Todd when we get back today."

"I will have my boat back by the end of the week," said Robert. "I'm looking forward to taking you all out on it."

Corinne clapped her hands together. "Oh! Are you sure?"

"I'll be anxious to get back on the water myself," he answered. "It's been three weeks. I'll be forgetting how it is done."

"I doubt that," said Mattie.

"I am going down to my son's tomorrow. I'll spend the night and bring the boat back the next day. After that, whenever you'd like to go out, just let me know."

Julie felt her stomach tighten, but she held her tongue and smiled.

Chapter 33

"I want to walk down to the water while the tide is out," said Mattie. "I love the feel of the wet sand, and watching those — what are they called, sand crabs? — burrow into the sand. Anyone up for joining me?" They were relaxing on the porch as the sun sank low in the sky behind them.

"I think I'm done for the day," said Edna, yawning. "I'm going to curl up in bed with that book I got at the aquarium. The photos are amazing. Such intriguing creatures."

Robert stood up and moved toward the steps. "If we're real lucky," he said, "we might find a treasure."

Julie and Corinne watched as Robert and Mattie walked down the stairs and out onto the sand.

Corinne reached her hand out and touched Julie's arm.

"He's a good man, Julie."

Julie turned to her, startled.

"What do you mean?"

"Mattie has been alone for a long time."

Julie answered sharply. "She's been happy, hasn't she? What has changed all of a sudden? I don't know her any more. Where is my Aunt Mattie?" Julie covered her face with her hands.

"Don't you see, Julie? Mattie spent nearly thirty years taking care of you, and then you flew away. She didn't try to stop you, but it left a hole in her life. That was okay for a while, but then she saw a way to start filling that hole with new experiences. Sailing! It was, like — well, The Blue Wildebeest — it was all out of context, but it was exciting."

"She's seventy years old. Why does she need excitement all of a sudden?"

"Why does anyone? Maybe excitement is too strong a word. But we all need something to keep us growing. Otherwise we start dying. No matter what our age."

Mattie and Robert had reached the waves, and were wading ankle deep.

"I can still see Edna falling into the water," Julie said. "I thought we were losing her. We did almost lose her." Julie's voice turned from distress to anger. "Way too much excitement. It's not worth it."

"Edna thought it was worth the risk. And I don't think she's sorry. Sorry for putting you and the rest of us through a scare, yes, but for herself, she has no regrets."

"Edna has always been reckless, I guess. But Mattie was always sensible. And you have been too. Suddenly, nothing makes any sense any more. Like you said, it's as if the world has become The Blue Wildebeest."

Suddenly Julie jumped up from her chair, looking toward the water. Mattie stumbled as a larger wave hit her knee. Robert caught her and held her close for a moment.

"It's okay, Julie." Corinne put her arms around the younger woman. "Don't be so frightened."

Julie sobbed and sank down into the chair.

"That man — that man . . ." she stammered.

"Yes — that man! She doesn't know it yet herself but Robert has made Mattie aware of things she had forgotten for a long time. Why does that scare you, Julie? Do you need to keep her to yourself forever?"

"She is making a fool of herself. She's not sane. Or she is senile. Why can't you and Edna see what I see? I know her better than you. I love her and can't bear the thought of losing her. All over a damn sailboat! I never want to see another one, or hear the word again."

Julie ran into the house, leaving Corinne shaking her head.

Later, the others having turned in for the night, Mattie and Robert sat alone on the porch.

"How many children do you have?" Mattie asked.

"Two. A boy and a girl. Miriam, the oldest, lives in Boston. She's not married. Bright, successful, compassionate, she's a lawyer for a non-profit advocacy firm. She comes and spends a few days or a week with me often. We usually all get together for holidays with Tom and his family."

"Your son? Are there grandchildren? "

"Three. A girl, 14, and boys 17 and 10. They were all still pretty young when Mary died. She only saw Seth as an infant. She would have enjoyed watching them grow up. They are good kids."

"The oldest one must be about ready to graduate from high school."

"Next year. He already plans to attend college and study marine biology. He doesn't know where yet. He knows the oceans are in trouble. He worries about it, and he wants to help fix things while there is still time."

"And the girl?"

"Heather's very athletic, and a good student too. But right now, her main interest is music, movies, make-up, and the boys!"

"She sounds pretty normal."

"She is. They all are, thank God. I know families that are not so lucky."

Julie was spending another sleepless night. She knew "they" were out there in the night, talking to each other — about what? What would two old people who barely knew each other talk about? In her mind, she heard Edward answer.

"What do young people talk about when they are new? What did we talk about, Julie?"

But that's different, she thought.

"Is it?" she heard in reply.

Once more she found herself lost in The Blue Wildebeest, everything strange and out of place.

"Mattie, please come home," she said out loud. But Mattie disappeared into the jungle, following a dark, heavy shouldered form.

Chapter 34

Wednesday dawned overcast and windy. The women were all glad to stay in and relax for the day. They had been on the go more than they had planned. Edna found a jigsaw puzzle on the shelf, and set it out on the dining room table.

"Haven't done one of these for years," she said.

"Is it going to stay cloudy the rest of the week?" Corinne wondered.

"I'll almost be glad if it does," said Julie. "I feel like I could use a long rest."

"I won't even mind missing the evening sail tonight," said Mattie. "But I am looking forward to the festival on the weekend. I hope it clears up before then."

"Yes," said Edna. "Me, too. I'd like to spend some time there. They are supposed to have good music, and dancing overlooking the beach. And lots of traditional food — lobster rolls, scallops, cranberry cakes, even bouillabaisse. I hope they have some of that Portuguese food."

"I'm sure they will!"

"I haven't danced for so long, I'd probably break my leg," said Mattie.

"Art and I could only do a few simple steps, but it was always fun."

"Edward loves to dance. Often, I get tired and can't keep up. He'll probably be able to keep all of us busy. He says he'll be back tomorrow night."

"I wonder if Robert dances?"

"I really want to find something special to take home as a souvenir," said Edna. "I have no idea what, but maybe I'll find just the right thing at the festival."

"For me," said Corinne, "I want something that I can place on my patio. Something definitely from the seashore, which will look out of place in the desert, and remind me every day to do something different again."

"We'll have to look at that bucket list we made up when we get back home."

"What bucket list?" asked Julie. "You didn't mention that to me. What's on it?"

The three women looked at each other guiltily.

"Oh, just stuff," Mattie hedged.

Julie was instantly more interested. "What kind of stuff?"

"Umm . . ." said Corinne. "Well, we talked about going to the Kentucky Derby."

"Oh! That would be fun."

"We haven't looked into getting tickets yet." Mattie was relieved to have the conversation head in a safe direction. "It might take a while. There's probably a five-year waiting list."

"We'll have to start searching when we get home," said Edna.

Julie smiled. "As a kid, I used to dream about owning a horse that was running in the Derby, and sitting in a special box seat, drinking a mint julep. I didn't know what a mint julep was, but it sounded good at the time. And, of course, at the end of the race, we'd be in the Winner's Circle. Funny how a child's mind can build such clear pictures of something you really know nothing about. Anyway, I hope I'm included in that trip."

"Of course," said Mattie. "We definitely had you in mind for that one."

Julie smelled a rat. "And what else was on your list — that I wasn't included in?"

"Well, we talked about a trip to Colorado," Corinne said quickly. Mattie swallowed hard. This was too close to the truth.

"River rafting," added Edna.

"That can be dangerous."

"Only in the rapids. There are quiet stretches of water as well."

"What's on your bucket list, Julie?" asked Corinne.

"I don't know," answered Julie. "I never thought about it."

"But you are the one who brought it up!" scolded Edna.

"But, well — you wait till later in life. When you can see the things you might be missing. And you've already done most of what you wanted to do . . . already." Julie stammered through her thoughts.

"Why not start earlier?" asked Corinne. "Seems like you'd accomplish more in the end."

Julie smiled and walked to the door. It was raining lightly now, but the porch was covered and dry. "I don't know. Seems like Edward and I have stayed busy with just the necessities of daily life. I don't think we have time for bucket list activities yet."

"You won't ever have time unless you make plans and just do them," said Edna. "That's what we were doing. Not really staying busy, but just not even thinking about what we might like to do. I think — or at least I hope, that we've learned our lesson. Whatever we want to do, we'd better get done, sooner rather than later."

Julie turned around and looked at the three women. "You three are my family, and I love you more than anything. But I don't always understand you. Sometimes you scare me."

"Well, back to the weekend coming up," said Mattie. "Vendors set up on Friday and music starts in the afternoon."

By evening, it was raining hard. The puzzle was complete, the air was chill, and the women were all wrapped in sweaters. Mattie coaxed the fireplace into producing a warm bed of coals.

"Look, these must be for roasting hot dogs and marshmallows," said Julie, picking up a long, forked, metal rod from a corner by the fireplace. "But we don't have either."

"And it's too wet to go out and get any. That's a shame. Roasted marshmallows would be good."

"Well, let's think. We have red pepper, onion, mushrooms, and we could cut up that chicken breast. Put it all on the skewers, and fold it into tortillas when they're done."

Quickly, they were all busy in the kitchen. The chicken was put in the microwave to cook halfway, while the vegetables were cut into pieces. Everything was drenched in olive oil and spices, and soon they were seated around the fireplace again, each with a long skewer held into the flames.

"While we were planning, we saw that it rains a lot on the Cape, and I kept hoping we would hit the right time and have nice weather," said Mattie. "But it's nice to see what a rainy day is like here, too."

"Art and I always planned at least one 'just doing nothing' day when we traveled. It was nice to see all the sights, try new things, but every vacation really had to include rejuvenating ourselves, and a day with nothing planned did the trick. That's why we liked to cruise so much. There were built in days with nothing planned, but when we were in ports, we stayed on the go all day."

"You and Art must have seen the whole world," said Julie.

"Not quite, but we did a lot of traveling." Corrine's voice became wistful. "Something to keep us busy. There are so many wonderful places in the world. I think our favorite was probably anywhere on the Mediterranean coast. The most exciting was the safari in Africa. We even got to see a real Wildebeest," she said. "A whole bunch of them, in fact. They aren't pretty like most antelopes. Ungainly, misshapen, with shaggy necks and near bare butts. There were hundreds of them, all running full speed. It was quite a sight."

"How did you and Art meet?" asked Julie. "I've never heard any stories about your background. You and Art were always so — I don't know, just so stable."

Corinne laughed, turning the long skewer over in her hand. "I guess you could call it that. Or just boring. We didn't have much excitement in our lives. Guess that's why we traveled so much. We used to call it getting away from it all, but really, it was more like we were looking for 'it' all the time."

"Did you grow up together?" asked Julie.

"We met our senior year in high school. Art's family had just moved into our small town, and he and I became a couple right away. We went to college together, got married after two years. I finished a secretarial degree and worked while he completed his bachelor's. We both looked forward to having a family, but it just didn't happen."

There was silence as the odor of roasting peppers filled the air.

"You'd have made wonderful parents," said Julie.

"I like to think so. It left a hole in our lives. So whenever we had a chance, we took off for places new and different." She paused briefly. "All three of us will be glad when you and Edward bring a baby into the family. He — or she — will be one spoiled child, with three lonely old aunts hovering around."

"How are we going to hover when you are 2000 miles away?" asked Edna. "You may just have to move to Phoenix, Julie."

Julie smiled wryly. "Don't be in a hurry. There is a lot of time yet."

"For you, maybe. But you keep reminding us that our time could run out fast if we aren't careful. I'd like to spend a lot of time cuddling a new baby, but I'd also like to see him grow up."

Julie looked around slowly at each of the women, then suddenly stood up, lifting her skewer and inspecting the charred morsels on the end. She said nothing.

"I'm sorry, Julie," said Edna. "Of course, it's not something you do for the old maid aunts. I was just joking."

Julie walked to the window and stared out into the rain. After a moment, Mattie got up and went to her side, placed a hand on her niece's shoulder.

"Julie. What is it?"

Julie turned and faced them. There were tears in her eyes. Finally, she sat down again, the skewer still in her hand. She looked at each of them in turn, then stared into the fire a moment. Her voice was soft, almost a whisper. "I never thought of that. You will be my baby's family, just as you have always been mine. The only one I've had." She turned to Mattie. "What if you weren't there?"

Movement in the room stopped, and the silence became thick. Mattie put her arms around Julie, and pulled her close.

Edna stared into the fireplace. Corinne pulled her skewer from the fire and rotated it slowly in front of her.

Suddenly, loud footsteps sounded on the porch. The front door flung open, and Edward entered as if blown by the wind.

"Hello, ladies! It's wet out there! I was able to get away this afternoon instead of waiting till tomorrow. Charlie picked me up at the airport." He hung his wet coat on the rack as he was speaking, then turned to face them. "Hmmm. It smells good in here. I hope you've made enough for me. I'm starving."

Julie crossed the room and hugged him tightly. "Of course," she said. "And I think it's time for the fajita wraps."

They sat around the table with savory chicken and vegetables spilling out of warmed tortillas.

"Seems as if you have had a cozy, rainy-day respite — from activity and worry. How are you feeling, Edna?"

"Fine," she answered. "In fact, I'll have to admit I feel better than I have for quite a while. I was tiring easily, and often felt out of breath, pressure in my chest. Lesson learned."

"Did you get the plane reservations changed?"

"All set for a week from Sunday. The doctors said that they would clear me for travel by then. They have sent all my records to my doctor and he's to set up an appointment with the cardiologist he wanted me to see before we came."

"And what do you all have planned for the next week?"

"Well, I was going to talk to Todd and see about getting on a sail boat," said Mattie. "But Robert has offered to take us out on his boat next week. We still haven't accomplished what this trip was all about."

"I think we should do it as soon as possible," said Edna, "to allow for any other unexpected postponements."

"You aren't planning any more excitement, are you?"

Edna just smiled and shook her head. "But, you know — the weather could stay like this all next week."

"It wouldn't dare," said Corinne. "It's going to be all sunny by Friday for the festival."

Edward turned toward Julie. "You are awfully quiet, sweetheart. Something in mind for tomorrow?"

"Well, with the rain, it would be a good day to see the Kennedy Museum. Probably terrible crowded, but everything is. We could wander around the shops and maybe even do the evening cruise if the weather clears."

"That sounds like a pretty full day, but we can stop if we get tired. I think we should go have breakfast with Ruthie. We haven't been there for a few days. How is Robert? He should not have missed this meal."

"He was going to his son's yesterday," Mattie answered. "He said he would be bringing his boat back tomorrow, unless the weather held him up."

"There sure aren't any boats to be seen out there today," said Corinne.

"There must be some pretty good waves coming ashore some places. Our beach here is pretty secluded, and look at those waves against the rocks."

Julie dreamed again that night. She saw Mattie, Edna and Corinne all together in a boat, floating on a calm sea. But they kept drifting farther and farther away. Julie was running along the beach, trying to keep them in sight, but they were waving to her and she could hear them laughing over the sound of the breakers. The sand was wet, and her feet sank into it. She struggled to keep moving, but her steps grew slower and slower, until finally she cried out and fell to her knees as the boat disappeared behind a wave.

Edward woke up at the sound of her cry, and folded her into his arms. "Wake up, sweetheart. What is it? You're okay."

"No! They're going. I can't reach them. I can't catch them." She sobbed against his chest. He rocked her and spoke soothingly, and she began to relax.

"Just a dream," he said. "It's okay now."

Julie pulled away and sat up on the edge of the bed. "Yes," she said. "Just a dream." Then she turned back to face him, stared at him wide-eyed. "But it's not a dream, is it, Edward? I can't make them stay forever."

Chapter 35

Thursday afternoon Robert called and said he had returned without the boat. "My son will bring it around as soon as the weather clears. Have you kept dry with all the rain?"

"We enjoyed the Kennedy Museum this morning," Mattie told him. "And we've been getting good use of the fireplace. If you'd like to come over and visit awhile, bring some marshmallows. We have a nice bed of coals and there's some chowder left from lunch." She turned to the others after putting her phone down. "Robert said he'd bring makings for s'mores, so let's keep those coals hot."

"I hope he will be able to tell us about the festival," said Corinne. "What time we should be where, etc. Rain plans if needed."

Robert arrived with a flyer describing the festival events and a time schedule in his hand, along with chocolate bars, marshmallows, and graham crackers.

"Milk chocolate for your sweet-tooth, or 85% dark cacao if you want real flavor. My favorite." He handed Mattie a bag with the makings, then turned to Edward, and held out his hand. "Did you have a good trip?"

"Yes. And how was yours?"

"I got to spend the day playing games with all three grandchildren. That used to happen regularly when they were little, but once they became teens, they are rarely all at home at the same time. My son, Tom, and his wife, Susan, were home, too, so it was a pleasant, mellow day with the whole family. How did you spend your rainy day, ladies?"

"Jigsaw puzzles and roasting kabobs in the fireplace," said Edna. "We took it easy for a day. Tell us about the festival."

"Tomorrow, vendors will set up in the town square early. Antiques, historical memorabilia, some really nice art work, and, of course, lots of souvenirs."

"I'm ready to do some shopping," said Corrine. "I haven't bought a thing to take home. Everything has gone into my stomach."

"The food vendors are wonderful, too, and there's music all day. Weather permitting, there will be some water events in the cove, as well. Fishing and sailing, probably some jet skis and para-sailing."

"And what is saved for Saturday?" asked Edward.

"More of the same in the square. The smorgasbord Saturday night will feature every kind of traditional Cape Cod fare: sea food, potato chips, cranberries, Portuguese, you name it and it will be there. I'd like to take all of you to it as my guests. I've already reserved a table." He held out a handful of tickets.

"That sounds wonderful," said Corinne.

Julie was quiet through the evening. She kept looking back and forth from Mattie to Robert. They all laughed and recounted the things they had seen over the past week, and what they would do with the unexpected time they would have for the next week.

"I'd be glad to pick you up tomorrow to go to the festival," offered Robert.

"We should probably take both cars," answered Edward, "in case some of us want to stay longer than others."

"Or go earlier," said Corinne. "I hope to find the perfect souvenir there. The vendors will be there both tomorrow and Saturday?"

"If we shop with the vendors during the day tomorrow, the evening activities will probably be enough for Saturday," said Mattie. "The slower pace has been nice this week."

"What time is the smorgasbord?"

"It starts at seven o'clock," answered Robert, "followed by music and dancing till everyone goes home."

Chapter 36

The town square, paved with cobblestones and shaded with red cedars and sour gum trees, teemed with vendors and shoppers when Mattie and her friends arrived the next day. Tourists, sampling savory soups and sandwiches, clustered around tables between the food vendors. Musicians — jazz, bluegrass, rock — took turns rotating onto the stage. The boardwalk next to it provided a dance floor. Beyond, a wide stairway led to the beach, where children splashed in the waves and built castles in the sand.

They selected items from several food vendors, then found a table with enough empty chairs for them all.

"Perfect for souvenir hunting," said Corinne, looking around. "I want something for my patio. Something out of place in the desert, but I want it big enough to be noticeable. Maybe a foot or so tall," she said, demonstrating the height with her hands. "Anything taller would be too hard to get home. But I want it to remind me of this trip every day."

"I'm not sure what I want," said Edna, "but I'll know it when I see it."

"Just memories," said Mattie. "I picked up a few shells at the beach. They will remind me. But maybe I'll find something else, too."

"Well, this is the place to look. Unless you are awfully hard to please," said Robert.

When the lobster rolls and bowls of kale soup had disappeared from their table, they wandered among the sellers and entertainers. Mattie found a dealer who specialized in antique nautical items, reverently touching several items while Robert explained their use and history.

By midafternoon, Corinne was carrying a foot-tall replica of the lighthouse they had climbed up into the first day they had explored the coast.

"Just what I wanted," she said. "And it includes a book with the history of the lookout, and stories surrounding it. Doomed love stories and shipwrecks!"

Edward and Julie bought matching Cape Cod souvenir hats and a set of six fish-shaped chowder bowls. "I'll never eat chowder again without memories of Ruthie's café," said Julie, and Edward agreed heartily. They were nearing the last few awnings and booths, when Robert drew them inside one. "Don't miss these," he said. "This fellow is nationally known for his wood carvings. Museum quality pieces."

"And prices," observed Mattie, fingering the tag on a beautifully detailed rendition of a whaling vessel.

Edna slowly moved further into the space, marveling at the intricately carved pieces, and subtle wood grains used in bowls and candle sticks. She stopped at a table of lifelike animals of different species and sizes. In the middle of the display, next to a dainty gazelle, was a large ungainly looking animal.

Its massive head had horns that curved up, out, and then inward. The neck and shoulders were bulky and heavily maned. The body narrowed behind the shoulders, sloping to a rump that might have belonged to a much smaller animal. The legs looked too slender to support the overall weight.

"Almost looks like a mistake, doesn't it?" remarked Robert. "An animal put together out of left-over pieces."

Edna chuckled, then reached out to lift the misshapen, yet beautifully carved creature.

"Look!" she cried, turning to the others as she cradled it in her arms. "It's a wildebeest!"

That evening, they ate Portuguese kale soup out of fish chowder bowls, with a lighthouse and a wildebeest at the table with them.

Chapter 37

The smorgasbord on Saturday evening was all that Robert had promised. Heavy with seafood prepared every way imaginable, along with beef, chicken and pork dishes. Vegetables of all kinds, roasted, steamed and fried. Salads, sauces and deserts featured cranberries, while bowls of locally made potato chips were on every table.

"Well, Edna, we'll have to thank you for arranging these extra two weeks for us. Without your mishap, we would not have been here for this feast," said Edward.

"It's not possible to sample everything," complained Corinne. "How do I decide what to leave out?"

"Come back next year," suggested Robert. "And the year after. Eventually you'd settle on a few favorites, but there's always something new on the table."

By the time the food was cleared away, people were beginning to dance in the square to swinging music. Edward and Julie soon joined them. Robert held out his hand to Mattie.

"Do you like to dance?" he asked.

She smiled and took his hand. "A hundred years ago, I did."

His hand in the middle of her back felt warm and electric as he guided her out onto the dance floor. He turned her toward him, and began to move with the music. As he drew her into a gentle embrace, her feet faltered.

"It's a waltz," he said. "Like this."

She pretended it was the dance step that made her hesitate, let him show her the simple movements, took a deep breath. "I remember now," she said, and allowed herself to relax into his confident arms. Soon they were moving as if they had danced together for years.

He drew her closer to him as the music neared the end, and she looked up at him.

"Thank you, Mattie."

She tried to smile, to answer thanks in return, but her throat was paralyzed.

Returning to the table, she sat down and reached for her wine glass, avoiding the eyes of her friends.

Robert remained standing. "Edna, are you up for a spin?"

They moved away, leaving Mattie and Corinne alone at the table. Julie and Edward had not returned.

Mattie recovered herself. "He's a good dancer," she said. "I seem to have forgotten a lot."

"Looked like you were keeping up nicely."

"Was I? I felt rather awkward."

"You didn't look awkward — and neither did he."

"The last time I danced was at Julie and Edward's wedding. And that was just a few circles around the floor. This seemed very different."

Corinne smiled. "Yes," she said. "I imagine so."

Julie and Edward returned to the table and sat down. It was getting dark, and the moon had risen. When the song changed, Edward took Corinne out onto the dance floor. Julie reached over and squeezed Mattie's hand, smiling. "Are you happy, Mattie? I'm so glad it's all turning out well. But we really can't go home without sailing again, can we?"

Surprised, Mattie squeezed Julie's hand in return.

"Julie, this trip has been so much more, and also so much less, than I had imagined. The world seems like a different place. We seem like different people. We've grown. At least I have."

"I have too, Mattie. Or rather I am — growing. It's not easy."

The others returned to the table, and Robert invited Julie to dance. She rose from the table slowly, tense and awkward, but as she felt his hand close around hers, and his hand on her back, she found herself relaxing, feeling no sense of threat.

"I'm glad the rain moved out," she said. "The weather's been perfect for this festival. Except for Wednesday and Thursday, it's been perfect the whole time we've been here."

"You chose a good time to come. It could have been different. Sometimes it rains for a week."

"We'll need to get Mattie on her sailboat ride before we are done."

"My son will get the boat returned in a couple of days."

Again, Julie felt her throat constrict. She steeled herself and answered, "I've had enough boating, but the others would like that."

Conversation flowed easily through the evening, wine glasses were filled over and over, and they rotated on and off the dance floor. The crowd began to thin, eventually, and Corinne was the first to yawn.

"The wine is beginning to put me to sleep," she said. "We should all sleep well tonight."

Robert stood up and reached for Mattie's hand. "Just one more," he said, and they moved into the crowd on the dance floor. He guided her across the square, toward the steps that led to the beach, then, with his hand still on her back, moved down the steps.

"It's a beautiful moon," Mattie said, looking up. Wisps of cloud layers took turns trying to hide the silver globe.

Robert stopped walking and stood still.

"Mattie," he said softly. She stopped breathing.

"Mattie," he said again. "I need to say something, but I don't know how. There isn't much time."

She turned to face him, but kept her eyes averted.

"I'm so glad . . ." he started.

"I wish . . ." he tried again.

"You live so far away . . ." he stammered.

He put his hand under her chin, and lifted her face toward his. "Do you understand?"

She nodded. She understood.

She was glad . . .

She wished . . .

But she lived so far away . . .

Robert put his arms around her, and drew her close to him. She felt her cheek against his collar, and, for a long moment, they were still.

"I'd like to take you sailing with me," he whispered. "Just the two of us. Could we do that?"

"Yes. Of course," she whispered. She looked up at him. "Of course," she repeated.

The music stopped, and he drew back, took her hands, and met her eyes.

"We don't have much time," he said. "Let the others go back to the house. I'll show you a wonderful place where we can sit on the beach — all night if you'd like." He hesitated. "It's just next to my place."

Mattie felt a myriad of ropes and shackles break loose and fall from around her. She laughed softly, and hugged him tightly. "We can't waste a moon like this, can we?"

"Ever since that first day, when you twisted your ankle, and I helped you back to the house, I've wanted to hold you in my arms again. I suppose Julie was right to suspect my intentions. Did you know?"

She shook her head. "Not then. It took a while for me," she said. "It was so strange — unexpected. But I know now."

They walked back across the dance floor and approached their companions. One by one, the four at the table froze as they caught sight of the two approaching them, arm in arm.

Mattie looked at her companions each in turn, then smiled a big smile. "You go on back to the house," she said. "I'm going with Robert for a while. I'll talk to you tomorrow."

There was nothing more to be said. Mattie picked up her purse and jacket, and leaned down to kiss Julie on the cheek. She turned back to Robert and they walked away, hand in hand.

Edward put his arm around Julie, whose face was drained of all color.

"Well!" breathed Corinne after a moment. "A lovely couple. Though a bit abrupt with announcements."

"I thought they were going to pass — in spite of Jake's invitation." Edna was smiling.

"Julie," said Edward, squeezing her to him. "Can you let her go?"

Julie smiled through tear-filled eyes. "She let me go," she said. "She never tried to stop me." She wiped the tears away with a napkin, and raised her glass in a toast. "It's time to attend my own bucket list. She looks happy, doesn't she?"

The Blue Wildebeest

The End

About the Author

Helen Sperber lives in Western Colorado near ski slopes, the Colorado National Monument, and the desert canyon country of Utah. She enjoys exploring the challenges and opportunities faced by women after transitioning from family-centered, nurturing years into the freedom to develop personal creative interests and talents. She holds a BA in psychology (University of Minnesota) and an MA in pastoral studies (Loyola New Orleans.) She has worked in pastoral care, as the activity director of a nursing home, and as a newspaper reporter. Her work has appeared in *Sanskrit*, *Diverse Voices Quarterly*, *Meridian Anthology of Poetry*, and *Front Range Review*, as well as local publications. *The Blue Wildebeest* is her first book.

*For bookclub discussion questions, recipes and more,
visit www.helensperber.com*

Lightning Source UK Ltd.
Milton Keynes UK
UKHW021148090120
356646UK00012B/1143/P